I0679030

The Keys,
And Other Short Stories

Charles Schwend

Published by
Quill To Book
Publishing

The Keys,
And Other Short Stories

Copyright 2016
By
Charles Schwend

Covers Copyright
2016
By
Charles Schwend

Charles Schwend may be contacted at: www.charlesbschwend.com

Quill To Book Publishing may be contacted at: www.quilltobookpub.com

ISBN: 978-0-9966512-2-6

Other Books Written by
Charles Schwend

<u>Dragon Dreams</u> – A beautiful young woman; An intimidating old man; An ugly dragon; A mysterious sword; A mythology from the dawn of time. All challenge the sanity of an unwilling young sailor selected to become the leader of a secret organization that is over two thousand years old. While stationed at an old Kamikaze base, he saves an old man, with a secret life, from a frozen river. His valiant rescue empowers him by ancient mandate, to become the Master of the White Ninja, a position he does not understand, nor want. The story is a tapestry of myth, love, danger and death. Dragon Dreams will capture an open mind in a novel of historical fact and mythological accuracy. This is not a book of martial arts.

<u>Words To Read, A Collection of Short Stories</u> – A colorful, insightful, collection of 23 memoirs, stories and one poem, based on recollection, legend and fantasy. The writings stem from Schwend's experience in the U.S. Navy, hobbies, family, and observing the world around him. Fantasy and a vivid imagination provide the mental stimulation for the remaining words to entertain an inquisitive mind. The short stories are from true memoirs, observation, whimsical half truths to full out fictional whim.

<u>Gulag #7, The Authorized Biography of Karl Lawrenz</u> - A gritty account of Karl Lawrenz from

birth in Pomerania, Germany to his current retirement as a U.S. Citizen, living in Highland, IL. This book is about his life and internment in a Siberian Gulag (POW camp) during WWII when he was 15 years old. He nearly died many times from starvation and illness. After WWII he continued to suffer under the harsh Russian rule of slave labor. He credits God for his life; his wife Inge, for the happiness found in his life; and the U.S. for the quality of his subsequent life. Some memories are a little grey. Karl cannot be one hundred percent sure that all his recall is without error. Some may not be remembered for a reason, or a purpose.

The Magical Switch – Originally written for a poetry contest sponsored by Famous Poets Institute and won an Honorable Mention from over seven thousand entries. The poem was written for a bedtime reading to assist young children to overcome their fear of sleeping in the dark. The book illustrations were made by Nicole Dormeier.

The Palace of Virtual Reality – A Professor Hamlock, head of a university science department, discovers how to bring holograms to life. Merlin the magician is the first to be re-created, followed by Aphrodite and other Greek Gods. Murder, lust, adventure and mystery soon follows.

Words, An Anthology of Short Writings - Editor of and Contributing Author.

A Dark and Stormy Night – Contributing Author

Table of Content

Dedication

This book is dedicated to my wife, Dolores, who suffered through the many hours of my cursing all word processing software, and computers in general, when frustrated by the lack of their logic flow consistency and not understanding what I wanted done.

The Keys

A board-end suddenly pops up, tripping me while examining my latest purchase. My nostrils fill with the accumulated dust that became airborne when I belly flopped onto the floor. Angry from my clumsiness, I kick the protruding board only to hear a cry of pain coming from me. Hopping on the uninjured foot, I chastise myself for doing this dumb thing. Loosing my balance, my face makes contact with the dust covered attic floor again. Tears flow from my eyes, making craters in the deep residue of time. I remain stretched out on the floor, waiting for the pain to leave my nose, which I just know is broken.

Sneezing from the dust coating my sinuses cause more extreme pain. Opening my eyes I see a tangle of golden metal. My eyes focus while pushing up from the floor and I see that the tangle is a ring of brass keys lying in a floor cavite. A mix of large and small, some bright and shiny, some dull with a green patina, some ornately made, some crudely crafted. They are old, very old, and I cannot remember any locks that would accept these ancient artifacts, but I have not yet examined the basement. I am keeping that experience for last. Reaching in to retrieve my find, I then stand up on unsteady feet.

I slowly descend the steep stairway, hoping to find the water had been turned on. The trickle of blood dripping from my nose will need attention, and my hands and face can use washing. Brushing the dust off my clothes will be fine until I make my way back to the hotel. I think returning in the morning to complete inspecting this once proud mansion would be the right thing to do. Reaching the kitchen, I find some old washcloths and towels. The plumbing rattles and growls when the faucet is turned on. Smelly brown water gurgles out, followed with clean, fresh smelling water pouring into the sink. Gently I wash away the blood, and then hold the cold wet cloth to my upturned nose. After several applications of the cold, wet water, the pain and bleeding, to my relief, stops.

Returning to my hotel room, I shower and hit the sack early. Dawn's first light finds me searching the basement for a matching lock to a key on the ring. The eeriness, of this supposedly haunted ancient home, makes the hair on my neck stand up, and goose bumps on my arms push out feeling like large grained sand on wet skin. Everything is like a bad omen, or even a forewarning against my current endeavor.

Relief that I had the foresight to have the power turned on does little to alleviate my pounding heart. Searching this ominous space would be a terrifying experience with only a flashlight to illuminate the secrets hidden in the nooks and crannies of this foreboding place. A door that appeared to look like an empty shelving unit reveals itself when turning a corner of the wall. There is no knob or handle, just a finger recess. Little effort is required to swing open the unit, revealing a staircase descending into a dark abyss. A high pitched squeal sounds a warning against trespassers. There is no switch in or outside the doorway, only an oily torch and self-igniting matches, nestled in holders on the wall. Striking a match on the cobbled wall produces a flame to ignite the torch.

At the bottom of the stairs is a massive timbered door with two enormous locks, above and below a huge wooden handle. Two of the keys from the ring, unlock the door. Stuck from years of non-use, the door only opens after great exertion. Cold, damp, and foul air that pushes out from behind the door produces an unearthly howl, bringing a fog like airborne plasma with it. An uncontrollable breath puts me into a temporary trance-like state and leaves me with a sweet, and acidy metallic taste.

The floor at the bottom of the stairs is hidden in a blackened void. Debating with myself whether I should proceed downward is pushed aside with an unexplainable curiosity. My descending footsteps echo to what seems to be infinity. The further I descend, the colder and heavier the air becomes, making my breathing like trying to overcome a soaked blanket covering my face. Niches along the stairway resemble ancient catacomb burial cavities. The dampness of the air runs down my body in rivulets filling my shoes. I am living a nightmare with no control over my destiny.

12

The bottom of the stairs that looms ahead rest on moss covered stone blocks partially embedded in a slime covered rock floor. Cautiously stepping out, trying to see what kind of room I have found, a large rectangular space opens to my vision. A large panoramic mural depicting human sacrifices and mass killings of war, is vividly portrayed on the far wall above five doors. The doors are made of timber with barred openings in the upper half. The light from my torch does not penetrate deep enough into the rooms to reveal what they contain. Deciding to enter the rooms to satisfy my curiosity, I begin with the first room to my left. The first two and the last two rooms are dungeon cells with shackles and drainage trenches that lead to an opening at the bottom of the back walls. The center room appears to be some kind of a storage area, filled with dry rotted wooden boxes with contents that have turned to dust many years before. The boxes at the rear wall had collapsed to reveal another locked, solid timbered door. One of the keys on the ring unlocks the nearly immobile door. The echoes of protesting frozen hinges reverberate through the room. Pushing with all my might slowly cracks the door open an inch at a time. Dank, musty air attacks my sense of smell. I cannot tell if I must

13

sneeze, cry, blow my nose or wipe the tears from my eyes first. A sneeze effectively clears both my nasal passage and my head.

A mind-freezing scene attacks my senses. Through an arched doorway is an adjoining room where sits five skeletons in five thrones; surrounded by chests filled with items of glistening gold and blackened silver, mixed with large multi-colored crystals. There is a sixth, empty throne that is clean as if waiting for an occupant.

Their rotted and shredded clothing hung from bones like grotesque confetti. Long golden rods are still held in clenched fingers and propped up against the thrones back. The slack jaws appear to be grinning at me, teeth stained with age. A light, source unseen, reflects a ghoulish glow on and around the setting. I notice that there are iron shackles chaining a leg bone of each skeleton to rings embedded in the stone floor. A warning comes to mind, to escape now to the freedom of the outside world. Thinking of the profits that could be made from this mansion and its contents forces me to continue with my investigation. Walking to an open chest of treasure, I pick up a jeweled broach made of solid gold. Forgetting the five occupants of the room, I randomly picked up exquisite pieces of jewelry and ancient coins that looks as if just recently crafted. Time is lost as I continue with my fascination. A deeper chill begins to permeate the room, alerting me to the passage of time. My watch reveals to me that it is now early evening. The whole day has passed without my realization. The sound of a closing door makes me jump up from a crouch, torturing my cramped muscles. Turning I see the door has slammed shut. Rushing to it I discover it is locked with no key access on this side. Looking around the door to find some kind of release or unlocking mechanism, I see a green brass plate mounted above in the stone. My stomach contents turned to acid as I read the words. "The keeper guardians of my bounty grow by the number of treasure hunters found."

A greenish cloud of gas drops from the ceiling and I slowly slide down the door to the floor. Awakening, I find myself sitting in the sixth throne, next to a new empty seat and I am chained to the floor. A smiling apparition appears and approaches me with a golden rod in its hands. I know that there is no rescue and greed is my downfall.

The Magical Coat of John Smith

It is cold, sleeting and windy. The low hanging roof only protects my upper body as I lean against the cold, wet brick wall. My life has become less than a basic existence since my once flourishing construction business failed. My accountant completely wiped me out and the total worth of my assets did not meet the financial obligations from the non-payment of bills.

I had contemplated suicide when the government informed me of the accumulated bills not paid. It took everything I had left to prove that the missing accountant had robbed me blind. I think that if I could find him, he would suffer horribly before his death.

Not many people are out on this miserable night. Exhaustion from my physical ordeal created a semi-conscious state. I think my mind and body are slowly slipping down to my own death.

A stranger stops before me, looking down, sorrow on his face. "Are you still alive?" He asks.

Slitting my eyes open I feel fever rack my body. Coughing I weakly answer. "Yes, I think so." My eyes painfully open up a little more to see the man remove his coat and gently cover me with it.

"Here, this will help. You should start feeling warmer now. Soon your body will heal and your mind become alert."

"Thank you sir, but I think this will only delay the inevitable. Tomorrow will be the same as tonight. Someone might come along and steal this fine coat from me."

"No," he said. "This is a magic coat, and will only perform it's magic once for you. You cannot be frivolous about asking for a magical event. Until then it will keep you warm and dry, impervious to theft or destruction. It will help you recover from your present precarious plight. Be warned that after your magical event happens, you must pass the coat along to another that needs its help. If you fail to comply with this one requirement within seven days, your life will return to

18

a worse situation than you are in now. Do you understand all this?"

"Yes. I believe so. I must pass this fine coat on to another in need within seven days of my receiving a great gift."

"Yes. That is about it. I must stress that you should be extremely deliberate about what you ask for. You cannot ask for anything that will harm another."

The man turns and walks away with the drenching sleet soaking his suit. The sleet stops and I get to my feet walking towards a diner. Having no money, I will try to get a bowl of soap by begging. Entering the diner, I start to say, "Could I please have a bowl ..."

The waitress watched me enter and walks toward the counter. "You poor man. You're soaked. Sit down and let me get some hot food into you"

"I don't have any money." I said.

"Don't you worry about that."

Turning to the short order cook standing behind the kitchen service window, she said, "Bill. Fix this man something hot to eat." and then placed a cup of hot coffee in front of me.

"Here is something to warm you until your food is ready."

"Thank you." My shoes and pants are already drying. I carefully take off my coat and gently placed it on the next stool. The frying food smells wonderful and makes my mouth water. I was on my second cup of coffee when the food arrived. Two eggs, hash brown potatoes, sausage and toast with jelly are gently placed before me.

The waitress stood smiling, across the counter, before me as I finished this magnificent food. "Can I wash dishes, sweep the floor or anything else to pay for this?" I asked.

"No dear. Your smile is enough."

I could not believe my good fortune. Getting up I left and crossed the street to sit on a bench facing the diner. What can I ask for, I thought. I have to be careful. A job would be good, or I could just ask for money. No asking for money is not good. A job would be best, but what kind of a job?

Thinking of what the best possibility would be, I noticed the friendly waitress walk out of the diner. She started crossing the street not noticing the oncoming bus. The bus driver would not see her because she is hidden from view behind tall shrubbery. I could tell she did not see the bus coming and the driver is not slowing down.

"Look out," I shouted, and started running across the street. I am thinking, "I wish the bus misses her." Reaching her before the bus, I pushed as hard as could away from the oncoming bus. I did not feel the bus hit me, but in my semi-conscious state a bright and opaque apparition, the man who gave me the coat, appears on the sidewalk, looking down at me with a smile.

I awoke to an EMT checking my vitals, and then asking me, "How do you feel? Can you move your arms and legs? Can you stand up? Do you think you need to go to a hospital?"

I answered, "Good, Yes, Yes and No." The waitress is telling everyone that I saved her life. The man who gave me the coat is gone, and the coat he gave me is gone.

The EMT helped me to my feet and again asked me how I felt.

"I feel fine." I said.

A man walks up to me and said, "I own the bus that hit you." Then handing me a business card says, "Here is my card. I own the largest bus company in the state. Come to my office tomorrow morning. I think I have a job for you." He then left.

I looked at the notation written on the card. "Peggy. Send this man right in to see me no matter what I am doing. There is a job waiting for him."

Time Travel Trader

The Mayan chieftain is pleased with the barter just completed. A large cache of royal pottery is made ready for transport. The Mayan is playing with the cigarette lighter he just traded for, fascinated with the flame that was sparked to life. "You should not use up all the magic. Use it only when needed," I said.

He carefully wraps the lighter and places it into the magic bag suspended from his shoulder. Smiling he turns and walks away surrounded by his entourage.

Entering my waiting time machine, I admire the soon to be ancient treasure before engaging the settings needed to return to the year 2016. My life has become very profitable, traveling in time and constantly trading up. A five-dollar lighter brings a hefty profit to me in my time. Museums and private collectors eagerly pay the price to purchase my wares. Precious jewels and metals are good for trading, but I have found that other, simpler items are more lucrative for trade in the past, present and future. The simpler items are also easier to track through time. Provenance can be convincingly engineered when documentation is secretly falsified and deposited in proper places to be found by researchers at a later date. Famous Jewels and hoards of precious metals have both an oral and written history that is harder to counterfeit.

I have been trading in time over five years, living an adventurous and rewarding life, but have come to realize that it is a very lonely existence. Security demands living a life without a close companion, where a slip of the tongue could result in a compromise of my secrets, or existence. My life is secretive, avoiding public notice and photographs. I have no record of past history and no family or other relatives associated with my name.

My walled estate contains a mansion, warehouses and workshops that are protected with a security system not yet known in the world. My house staff and workers are from different times and locations, loyal to me without a fault. They vacation back to their own time, and experience a god like rest once a year, bearing gifts unimaginable and from periods that their peers cannot comprehend. We all share a comfortable life from our endeavors.

I have in the past became involved with women that were brought by me to this time, but having little in common to share, the relationships soon dissolve. I will have to search in my own time for someone to share my life, thoughts and the fruits of my work.

Returning to my time, I turn the pottery over to my workers for cataloging and detailing a history to convince any expert of their authenticity. My senior maid, Mattie, from the early Clovis culture, and the woman of the house, greets me at the main entrance with a cup of my favorite coffee. Balancing the porcelain cup and saucer, I retire to my sitting room where soothing music relaxes my mind and body.

Mattie said, "Sir. A young journalist, a Miss Kerrie White, from World Informer Magazine, has called in your absence to request an interview about your life. I told her that you would not be available for an undetermined amount of time, but she was very persistent. She left her phone number and stated that she would be calling back every day until you are available. Shall I notify you when she calls again or ignore her future calls?"

"Yes Mattie. I'll take her call. It's best to culminate curiosity instead of intensifying the mystery surrounding it."

"Very well, Sir."

"And Mattie."

"Yes, Sir?"

"I think you should prepare an oriental meal for dinner. Do you have everything you will need?"

"I do indeed, Sir."

"Thank you Mattie. I don't know how I could function without you. Now I will take a short nap. It has been a tiring day."

Mattie dims the lights, then leaves, closing the door silently behind her with a Cheshire smile.

Daniel Biggs slowly drifts into a deep sleep, dreaming of past adventures in his life. His subconscious dwells on events of high excitement, moments of regret and dealings that were not finished to his liking. A soft knocking awakens him. Mattie enters the room and announces that the young journalist is calling again. "I'll take the call here Mattie," I said.

A sensual young voice came through the telephone, a very pleasing tone that was a joy to listen to. "Mr. Biggs, my name is Kerrie White and I would like to interview you about your life. I feel my magazine subscribers would enjoy reading about you. I have to tell you that after conducting a deep background search, I cannot find anything on you, while the leading antiquity authorities state that you are the most prolific discoverer of ancient artifacts in the world. Could I meet with you and enlighten my readers?"

Listening to Miss White stirred Biggs' loins. Her voice simmered a lust to his mind and body. "Well Miss White, I lead a very private life but would be willing to avail myself for a short interview. I could address your questions during dinner this evening. We could discuss what part of my life you would want more details in. Would that be soon enough for you?"

The excitement was obvious in her voice as she replied, "Yes. And what time would it be suitable for me to arrive?"

"I think the kitchen staff will be able to prepare everything for a 7:30 meal. If they have to run a little late or you arrive a little early, we can enjoy a drink while waiting. Bring your notes for an easier transition into the interview."

"Oh, that would be great. Would you mind if I record everything. I would not want to miss or misunderstand a word."

"Fine. The gate will open when you arrive, but do not be surprised when it closes behind you."

"Thank you Mr. Biggs. I promise that you will not regret giving me this opportunity."

"Goodbye Miss White. I will see you later this evening."

Ringing for Mattie, I asked her if adding a guest to dinner would create a problem. "Not at all Mr. Biggs. I always have extra prepared for any unexpected guests and the kitchen staff always makes good use of the left overs."

"Good, I told my young guest that we should be seated at 7:30 p.m."

"Very well Mr. Biggs." Mattie left the room with an obvious scowl on her face. I smiled at her over protectiveness, and then called Merle Caines, my head of security.

"Mr. Caines. There will be a Miss Kerrie White, a journalist from World Informer Magazine, coming to dinner tonight. I need to know everything about her before 7:30. Let me know what you find."

"Sure thing Mr. Biggs. Do you want hard copy or just a phone call?"

"A call will be fine, but prepare a hard copy for tomorrow morning, just in case I need to follow up on her."

Preparing myself a drink, I mentally constructed areas of my life where the interview could be easily steered to, prepared answers to any possible questions, and fantasized about this Miss White while wiling away the time.

The clock chimed seven o'clock when the driveway bell rang. 'She's early, but that's O.K. This will give me time to evaluate her intentions and how well versed her interviewing skills are. If nothing else, this will help hone my skills in deflection and misinformation. I always enjoy a challenge or a battle of wit before retiring.'

Mattie opened the door, and then coldly announced Miss White. Our telephone conversation did little to prepare me for her presence. Even Mattie had that cat eyeing a bird look as she escorted her in. She was breathtakingly beautiful wearing a simple black dinner dress. "I'm sorry Mr. Biggs, I forgot to ask about any dress code you may have for your dinners, and so I wore what I hope is appropriate."

"That is fine. We do not usually follow a dress code here, unless we are entertaining a formal affair. Personally, I prefer casual attire."

"I'll remember that."

"Mattie, would you inform the kitchen staff that my guest is here and they should serve whenever dinner is ready."

"Yes Sir. I am sure they'll be ready shortly"

"Well Miss White. Would you care for a drink while we wait?"

"Yes. A white wine would be nice if you have it."

"Anything you could possibly want is available here Miss White."

"Please, call me Kerrie."

"And I, Daniel."

Going to the wine cooler, I opened a sparkling semi-sweet apple wine. "I think you will find this apple wine a good choice to sharpen your appetite, Kerrie."

"I am sure your taste in wine is impeccable." Taking a sip produced a murmur of satisfaction. "That is an excellent wine. I do not recognize the label. Where is it from?"

"We produce our own spirits; Wine, cordials, brandies, whiskeys and even a few rums. After dinner we can sample a few." I said.

Mattie, with a momentary tight lip and chilly look, announced dinner and escorted us to the table. I seated Kerrie next to me, off to the side of the table head. She took in the antique settings, lifting a knife to examine it closer. "Excuse my rudeness, but this is beautiful piece for everyday use."

"This serving was a lucky find for me from one of my purchasing trips through the Baltic area. It is from an old family that was losing their castle through bankruptcy. I bought everything but the land."

The staff began assembling the first course at the serving station. "What is your kitchen preparing for us this evening? The aromas smell addictive."

"We are having trout with an oriental plum sauce and I believe dessert will be a cherry sherbet topped with a reduced sweet cherry cordial."

We enjoyed our dinner with Kerrie's complimentary comments. "Where does your staff find these recipes. I have never tasted anything like this. This is better than a five star restaurant."

"My staff can prepare any entrée from anywhere or from any time."

Following dinner I thanked the staff for their outstanding skills and then escorted Kerrie to the library. I took a seat at a large library table while Kerrie walk from stack to stack examining the exposed book spines, occasionally commenting on their titles. "These are really rare volumes. How did you manage to collect so many of them? Have you read all the books here?"

Laughing, I said, "I have been collecting for years. I wish I had the time to read all the books here. That is something to look forward to in my retirement. Shall we start on the interview?"

Her insight and intelligence surprised me, especially for a young journalist. Questions built on successive answers revealed a quick mind that followed the thread of her thoughts. I had to be very careful not to inadvertently reveal avenues to areas that needed to be closed off to her. It was late into the night when she started yawning with excuses for her apparent tiredness. "You could stay the night, if you wish, and we can continue this tomorrow at a more leisurely pace."

"But I don't have a change of clothing, or even night clothes. I never thought I would need them tonight."

"My staff can produce anything you may need from our storage closets. I have suites in another wing for unexpected overnight stays. Some of my business dealings can take several days, or more, to discuss and finalize. It would not be a problem." Then laughing, I said, "And we have very good door locks."

Kerrie stayed with me for a week. During breaks in the interview, I showed her some of my antique and coin collections. Her perceptive questions always turned to my past, where was I trained and how I found what I sell. "I have agents around the world, in every major city, listening for possible finds, investigating the most outlandish claims. Many of our major finds were based on rumor or myth. We reward informants and profit share down to the lowest employee.

We eventually shared a bedroom to both our delights, but even our pillow talk was centered on my ability to locate and procure treasures unknown until their availability for sale was announced. The house staff and estate workers fell in love with Kerrie, everyone but Mattie. We found shared interests with mutual philosophies on life. After the week, she left to collect herself, she said.

Three days after Kerrie left, I received a registered letter from one of the largest auction houses that handles a good percentage of my sales. "We have been served a court document requesting information on the provenance protocol used in authenticating your items in our care. Please be advised that we will do everything legally possible to maintain our claimed secrecy of our clients. Please inform us of any special areas that you wish to personally address. Sincerely."

I knew in my heart that my lust had overridden common sense in dealing with Kerrie. I replied to the auction house, "Please convey your provenance guidelines in response to the court document, but state that all other information requests has been referred to me. Also relay to the document server the name, address and all contact information of my legal firm and also my personal contact information. I appreciate your timeliness, informing me of this legal maneuver. Above all, do not put your company or yourself in any comprising light. You are a good friend and business associate. Yours Truly,"

I contact my legal advisers, informing them of the current intrusion into my business concerns, asked them to prepare a plan to counter this attack and to investigate the perpetrators and what their objective is.

Next I attempted to contact Kerrie through World Informer Magazine. "She is no longer with us." The senior editor said.

"My name is Daniel Biggs and I need to talk with her. Can you give me any contact information or if not, can you get a message to her to call me?"

"I do not have any telephone numbers or addresses for her, but I can put information out there for your need to talk with her. Yes, I can do that."

"Thank you."

Mattie knocked and informed me that Mr. Caines is here with an emergency. "Some entity attempted to penetrate our computer network trying to place malware in it. Our filter system caught and isolated the code. We are trying to backtrack to identify the source. Did you want to authorize a locate and destroy measure?"

"Yes, Mr. Caines. I would like to hear that you have burned their equipment, especially the hard drives. I hope you can accomplish this without leaving a trail back here."

"Consider it done, Mr. Biggs."

Next I began to develop a plan to gather intelligence the old fashion way, data assembly and deduction. Within thirty minutes Kerrie called.

"Daniel, I understand you need to talk with me."

"Yes, Dear. I will be going on a buying trip for some ancient Persian artifacts and was wondering if you would like to join me."

"Oh, I would love that. When will you leave and what will I need?"

"Tomorrow morning and you will need both tropical and heavier clothing for freezing weather, and your personal hygiene items, of course. Bring enough for a week to ten days travel. I will provide everything else. You may also want to bring a digital camera so you can record the marvelous scenes you are likely to see. I am planning on leaving around 8 a.m. If you want, you could come tonight and get a fresh start tomorrow morning." I almost heard her gears working. I could tell that she had covered the mouthpiece and was talking to someone.

"Yes, I would love to come along. Would it be O.K. if I got out there between nine and ten this evening?"

"That would work out great. I'll start making arrangements for you to join us. We will see you tonight."

Mattie came into the sitting room. "Sir. Did she fall for the trap?"

"Yes she did. And now you know what you will have to do tomorrow."

"Yes. I am to drive her car, dressed in clothes similar to hers, and park at the Super Mall in town where I will change clothes in a dressing room. Martin from the kitchen staff will follow me to the mall and return me here. Do you think it will fool her friends?"

"I'm sure it will Mattie. Now, what would you like me to bring back from Persia for you?"

"Oh, just anything. You know what I like, but nothing gaudy. Maybe you could bring me something made from ivory or a piece of sparkly jewelry."

"You can count on it."

Kerrie arrives shortly before 9 p.m. We are ready for her. Household staff went to the car and carried her travel bags to the foyer. Mattie escorted her into the sitting room where Mr. Caines and myself waited, then went to change and proceed to her assigned mission. "Kerrie. Please have a seat. This is Mr. Caines and we have a few questions for you."

"I don't understand. I thought we were to get ready for the trip."

"We will be ready, but first a few questions. First, whom are you working for? Secondly, what is your assignment? And third, how are you suppose to contact your handler?"

"I don't know what you're talking about." She said. "Daniel, what do you suspect me of? I just want to be with you. I am totally confused."

Knowing that she is really good at what she does, I decided to interrogate her later under a more controlled situation. "It's O.K. Kerrie. We just had to be sure of you. Try to forget this happened and we will continue on our trip, if you still want to."

"I do not know what has happened, but yes, I still want to go with you on the trip. I want to be with you."

The three of us enjoyed a few drinks and discussed possible events during our excursion. "Mr. Caines, has Mattie returned from her errand?"

"Yes, Mr. Biggs. "

"Good, we will continue with our trip." "Kerrie, did you bring your camera?"

"Yes, it's packed in my luggage."

"Great. I love it when a plan comes together. We had better get some sleep. Tomorrow is going to be a long day."

Breakfast brought more trip discussion. Mr. Caines and two more members posing as drivers went over travel plans, airline connections, ground travel and security traveling into Syria.

Escorting Kerrie and lugging her luggage to one of the out buildings we entered a steel door. Kerrie stood with mouth gaped open looking at the bank of electronic controls while I secured the door. "Daniel, what is this? I thought we would be going to one of your vehicles."

"This is a vehicle, a very special one. Please strap yourself into a chair while I prepared for take off."

"Take off? What is this? Where are the others?" She said while reluctantly strapping herself in.

"All in due time Dear."

Making settings for Persia in the year 950 BCE, I energized the machine, and then sat in the chair next to Kerrie. "We will be travelling in time to Persia where I will trade with the King's Court." A loud humming accompanied a mild vibration that lasted less than forty seconds. The air is filled with a warm fresh scent.

"Daniel, what are you trading? I don't see anything here."

"You my Dear. You are my goods of trade. I had shown a photo of you to the King and he is very desirous to add you to his harem, and he has offered golden statuary for you. I think I am getting the better deal. What do you think?"

I opened the steel door to the King and his attendants. Viewing Kerrie, he smiled and motioned his men to get her. "No Daniel, I will tell you everything. Please do not do this. Daniel, please stop this. There is a large organization wanting to get control of your company. You do not want to mess with them. They are killers who will do anything to accomplish their goals. I can help you."

"It is too late Kerrie. The deal has been struck. I think you will have a very luxurious life here." I watched her fight her captures, screaming curses as she and her luggage are carried off. Her struggles create a clothing malfunction, much to the delight of her escorts. Other men bring in the golden statues.

"These are old Gods that were honored by my forefathers, Gods that are no longer held in favor." The King chuckled. "I think I have received the better half of this trade. I have never seen one like this. Eyes that look like deep-sea water and hair the color of straw. She is young and will bear my family and I many children. Now if I can just keep my concubines from mutilating her out of jealousy from her looks. I thank you for showing me how to use this instrument you call a camera. I will use it to record her life for you. How long do you think she will live? When her usefulness is over, will you be able to replace her?"

"Maybe, we will have to wait and see."

Identity Theft Retribution

Darian Swanson sits in an overstuffed chair, not watching or hearing the television blaring across the room. He just recovered from another episode of PTS, a gift from the U.S. Army he received in the Persian Gulf. The bourbon sloshed out of the glass in his shaking hand. Less than a swallow remains after his mind manufactured the earthquake that ravaged his body. *I am getting better, I can remember the events and I'm still sitting in the chair. I need to clean up now and go somewhere public. I need some people around me. I need to see how normal people act. I need to get better, faster.*

Shaving slowly with a trembling hand, a vision of strolling to the nearby cafe plays out in his head. Fresh air bolsters his mind and body. He can now remember scenes of the war and not collapse. The walk and breathing in the crisp morning air stirs a hunger. After stepping in to order a freshly prepared breakfast, he enjoys his meal. Finished, he goes to the cashier, pulls out his credit card and swipes the reader. The screen reads "overdrawn". He stammers to the cashier, embarrassed, and then pays in cash.

Possible reasons for the overdrawn status are considered while returning home. None of them fit. He immediately calls the credit card companies when getting home. They all report that large purchases were made within a thirty-mile radius of his home. "You should contact your bank immediately. It seems your identify has been stolen. Your bank can put a stop on your accounts, just like we did. If you have other credit cards, contact them also. We are so sorry this has happened to you."

The bank representative is also sorry. "You should file a police report as soon as possible," she said.

The police are also sympathetic. They make copies of the purchases provided by the credit card companies. "Please keep me updated on what you find out from your investigation" I said. "This theft gives my life a purpose, but not one that I want."

The next day the police department calls requesting that I come down to the station. *They have information. Good, something is being done. I'll get this mess straightened out and maybe then I can re-start a normal life.*

Arriving at the police station, I am directed to a Sergeant Able. "If you would review these photographs taken at the time of purchase, you'll hopefully be able to identify the guy using your cards."

The scumbag is totally unknown to me. He looks like a grease-ball leering at the cashiers who are just out of the picture. Most of his activity was at the Wal-Mart just a few blocks from my house. "Can I have a few photos of that creep and a list of the his purchases?" I ask.

"No, not while the investigation is active," replies the Sergeant.

"Can I get a cup of coffee? All this is really getting me down. I need something to help me focus."

"Sure. I'll get you a cup of joe that's better than that vending machine crap. Wait here, I'll be back in a couple."

As soon as the Sergeant leaves the room I pick up a couple of the better shots and slip them into my pocket. Then furiously jot down the more expensive items he purchased. I am done by the time the Sargent returns.

Handing me a filled Styrofoam cup, he said, "Here, this is from the secretaries private coffee maker."

Calmly sipping the hot brew I engage in small talk about how much of my loss I can expect to recoup, the character of this type of thief, what percentage of them get caught and for how long they are normally incarcerated. None of the answers seem right to me. After finishing my coffee and the conversation, I return home to plan how I will take care of this maddening intrusion into my life.

I had observed in the investigation file that almost all the purchases were made during the busiest hours of the day, early morning and the evening rush. At five p.m. the next day I circle the Wal-Mart parking lot until a spot opens across from the main doors. The space is perfect for a stakeout and I am ready. Some of the customers give me a more than curious look as I pour coffee from a Thermos and use a pair of binoculars whenever someone resembling the man in the photos, enters or exits the store.

Nothing happens the first day, but the next morning I have him. I do not even need the binoculars. He comes strutting out of the store like he is untouchable. He is an easy surveillance and I follow him to his front door like reading a map. A visit with his neighbors produces his name, Tim

44

Brown, and a not so glowing report on his character. His activities are suspicious and the police have been to his house several times.

That night I drive past his house. There is only one car; no evidence of a wife and the yard is void of children's toys. The lawn and house are not maintained. No curtains in the windows, just shades. Everything looks in disrepair.

Parking two houses down from his, I pull some zip ties from my carefully prepared workbag and place them into a briefcase containing a small caliber handgun, a roll of duct tape and a stack of papers. Getting out of my car, I straighten my tie and suit coat, and then look over my dirty car and mud-covered license plates. It does not take much work to hose down the car and then throw dust over it, but not enough to make it stand out. Walking up to the house I knock on the door and then pull out a business card that I had previously and carefully prepared.

Footsteps approach the door that swings open and there that thieving son-of-a-bitch stands with a quizzical look on his face. "Yah, you need something?" he asks me.

"Are you Tim Brown?"

"Yah, who's asking," He said.

Handing him my card, I said, "Mr. Brown. My legal firm, Jason and Harrington represents the estate of Jack Smith who recently passed away without leaving any family members. After an in-depth record search it has been determined that you are his only living heir. There is a very substantial amount that needs to be dealt with. If you have a few minutes, I would like to come in and discuss what all this will entail."

A crafty look rolled over Tim's face. "Yah. What do I have to do?"

"Nothing."

"Then come in and kick any junk out of your way." He indicates for me to sit on his cruddy sofa. I sit without expression or a reflection of my disgust. A suspicious look is followed with "This going to cost me anything?"

"No. Not a cent, all expenses are covered by the estate. Even your future travel and meal costs will be covered. Ah, could I bother you for a glass of water? It's been a very long day and I am parched."

"Sure, wait a sec." After he leaves the room, I slip the zip ties out of the brief case and cover them with some papers. I remove the revolver and keep it at my side. Hearing his

46

return, I stand and point the gun at him as he comes through the doorway.

"Keep calm. I'm not going to hurt you. I just have some questions for you. Now sit down." I motion for him to sit in a straight back chair and then zip tied his wrists to the back.

"What the hell is this? What do you want?"

"Well Mr. Brown, my name is Darian Swanson. Does that ring a bell? I am here to get back my money that you stole from me. I have a list of merchandise you bought with my credit cards and I expect restitution."

Laughter echoes through the house. Trying to talk in-between his bouts of laughter Mr. Brown said, "You fool. All the money and junk are gone. Drugs, booze and women ate it all up. It's all gone and you can't get blood from a turnip."

"That was over $130,000. How did you spend that much in such a short time?"

Laughter again. "Well women cost and you don't get much for what I had. You might as well just knock me around a bit and cut me loose, cause your not getting anything here."

Pulling the roll of duct tape out of the brief case, I run it around his head, covering his mouth and eyes. He's fussing and kicking trying to get loose when I hit him over the head with an empty beer bottle that was setting on a cluttered coffee table.

I go through the house, room to room, looking for something valuable. There is nothing but dirty clothes and used drug paraphernalia. It is late and dark. Tim Brown is still out cold. Cutting him loose from the chair, I re-secure him with zip ties and more duct tape. All the surrounding houses are dark. I move my car to the front of his house, and throw Brown into the back seat.

It is dark and quiet at my house. Throwing the wriggling body over my shoulder, I take him down to the basement. There is an old single bed down there that I was planning to throw away. It is the perfect place for this dipstick. He starts to become more active, thrashing about. Ripping the duct tape off his mouth brought a lot of hair with it, followed by a piercing scream. "What the hell yah doing? I ain't got nuthen to give you. What do you want from me"?

"Satisfaction." I said. "I don't know if I want to do this fast and easy, painless to you, or slowly, piece by piece, to maximize your pain. I guess it will all depend on how the orders come in."

"Piece by piece, orders. What the hell are you talking about? You're crazy."

48

"Well, I was a decorated Army Medic, that went a little crazy over in the Persian Gulf and received a Medical Discharge. I was an Emergency Room Medic. Now I think body parts sales, on the black market, will get my money back and you are going to help."

"I am going to help? What… Oh no. Look, you don't have to do this. I'll get you your money. I'll get you anything you want. Don't do this."

I notice that my tremors are gone. Smiling, I pull my medical ER kit from the shelf and said, "Yes, I know I'll get my money." Opening my kit I check blades for their sharp edges, saws for correct pitch and my supply of anesthesia. "I'm sorry, but I'll have to tape your mouth again. Then I'll get on the computer and make some phone calls."

Another Life – Another Time

My long anticipated passing is disturbed by a crying newborn. My reincarnation is always male. I hope that this male is not my new entity because I do not want to be identified as a crybaby. My cycle of death and new life started at the beginning of time. It is a curse at the time of new life because of body changes during growth, and a curse at the time of death knowing the pains of death and new growth. My memories, intellect and physicality are compounded at each new beginning, when I must conceal what I am, to prevent identification, examination and dissection, from people less than myself.

My memories go back to my very beginning when fleeing for my life. Others in my clan realized that I was different and thereby not eligible to remain in their midst. Anyone showing a physical or mental tangent from the clan's norm was routinely eliminated. Experiencing many close calls since then evolved me to be quite adept at appearing as though a clone of them.

Many times in the past, my identity was fabricated to hide progressive intelligence and inventiveness. I have lived the lives of famous world leaders, scientists, heroes, religious leaders, military genius and even as a common family member. I always feel sadness, at the time of passing, for losing ties to family and friends that I cannot maintain in my new life without revealing what I am. Each new existence brings new challenges to achieve a better self and enhance my ethics. I am not now, or ever, been perfect. I have made many mistakes and have learned from each one. Some of my lives have been short while others extremely long. I have no preference for identity or social standing, knowing what will always come with time.

Suffering from longing for friends and partners past, I have become more selective in mentality and personality than physical attributes and wealth accumulated. Becoming a better person has become an instinctive striving in my psyche and I have become more comfortable with myself. My associates have no control for comparison to see or realize my change from life span to life span, while I feel in my mind and heart the ever-changing improvement in myself.

I see the upward improvement in the interactions of people, and countries, over the generations, that thwarts the need for power and wealth accumulation that generated past deeds of the monsters that are occurring less and less. I feel that some credit can be extended to me for these improvements, through advisement, counseling and occasionally example.

In my later reincarnations, I have become less passionate and attentive to the needs of the recipients, of efforts made to their enrichment of life, and feel that maybe my mission is coming to an end. I wonder what power made me what I am and if it will all end. Then what? Will I fail to become renewed? Will I simply no longer exist?

The light is starting to fade. Family and friends surround me to ease my passing, but mostly to make them feel more comfortable with my passing. The light turns dark to nothing.

My eyes open to see a young woman nuzzling me and making cooing sounds. The light is bright and I smile at my new life. My life is now comfortable – all except a wetness spreading below my waist and I start to cry from my new discomfort. I am again alive with a newness that is always challenging.

Cavemen

I was somewhere between thirteen and sixteen years old, working as a staff member at a Boy Scout Camp, in Sunnen Valley, just off Shirley, Missouri. One of the more popular events at the camp was exploring the cave. Campers were vigorously warned not to enter the cave without a staff member.

One day in the middle of the week after a group of five scouts had their initial cave experience, they decided to explore deeper into the cave, by themselves. Their initial orientation was following the creek and entrance passageway. They had penetrated the cave until just before the first major room. The great room had five entrances, and that meant there were also five exits. By not looking back to take notice of which entrance they used going into the vast cavern, they became lost, but not knowing that they were lost.

Later that evening, the missing scouts troop leader became aware of their absence. Questioning the other troop members revealed that they had been planning an unauthorized excursion into the cave. A staff meeting was quickly conducted and assignments given. The camp director notified the authorities, search parties were assembled and parents contacted. Of course, the news media learned of the emergency.

I was the youngest member of the staff, and as such was not assigned a responsibility in the recovery team. Being an adventurous soul, I decided to become a more accepted member of our staff by entering the cave before the organized search party and rescue the lost scouts.

Returning to my quarters, actually a two-man tent, I changed into throwaway warmer clothes and boots, checked my flashlight for new batteries and hiked to the cave entrance. I had experienced many prior trips into the cave, escorting small parties in and through the great room. Visions of recognition and accolade accelerated my pace.

I found the five scouts, all about my age, exploring the cavern, studying tall ghostly white bean sprouts growing in a small field where they apparently fell out of someone's pants cuffs onto the muddy floor. They were enjoying themselves, excited about their discoveries and did not realize that they were lost, until I told them. And yes, they did not know what passage returned them to the cave entrance.

They all wanted to further explore the cave beyond the great room; even after I told them they were not dressed for exposure to the cold damp air. They insisted on continuing further into the cave. Being hyped on my heroic save I agreed to take them further. Since I was now, I thought, such an expert authority on the Sunnen Cave, I agreed to take them further into the labyrinth. It wasn't too long before realizing that I was also lost and way over my head. We wondered through strange sights and mystifying sounds. Highway vehicle traffic was heard during one phase of our wondering and followed a footprint trail to a solid rock wall that was blocked off by a huge boulder that covered half of a print. The mud that held the prints was solidified. Messages written in carbide lamp smoke recorded exploration as far back as the early 1800's.

Flashlights became dimmer and the damp cold started affecting the scout's bodies. Some fell, skin bruised and cut, while others became separated only to reappear at a later junction. Mild hysteria set in during talk of dying and never being found. I tried to minimize the negative aspects of our situation, but found myself thinking the same way. We began rationing the use of our flashlights to conserve the batteries.

Finally, we thought we recognized some of the features seen walking through the tunnels. Excitement grew thinking we had found a way out. Then we thought we could hear someone shouting, but it wasn't from down any of the passageways. It was through a shallow horizontal crack in a huge rock shelf just wide enough for us to squeeze through. What seemed to be hours of crawling, but was actually just minutes, we were through the shelf and in the company of our rescuers.

Later, after hot cocoa and sandwiches, we learned that we had penetrated over five miles into the cave system. Further than anyone in the camp or any of our rescuers. All the news media carried the story, much to my embarrassment and the camp director was considering voiding my contract and sending me home. He reconsidered after protest from the majority of the camp staff.

In later years, when my son attended Camp Sunnen, stories were still being told of the six scouts lost in the cave. To my relief, no names were mentioned.

Midnight Hitchhiker

Shivers wake me as a cold breeze works its way over and around my body. A soft nuzzle caresses my cheek. A musty odor attacks my olfactory nerves and travels up through my sinuses, numbing my face and forehead. Before opening my eyes, I think that this is the dumbest thing I have done since high school – getting drunk in a cemetery with a bunch of idiots. Steeling myself for the pain, I open my eyes. Throbbing increases in intensity and colorful spots dance before my eyes.

It is dawn and I have to get ready for work. Hangovers are not tolerated in the service industry. One complaint and I will receive counseling and after the second complaint I will be out the door. I need this job for my sanity and livelihood.

Before she died, her father arranged this employment for me. Strings were pulled to make this happen. I guess my wild reputation preceded me, even though Mary Ellen cleaned me up after we met.

I read the name on the tombstone when I stand up on wobbly legs. Nope, don't recognize the name. Hell I can barely read the five-inch high letters. What the hell were we drinking last night? My clothes are filthy, my skin is gritty and there is grass and twigs in my hair.

Looking around, I can almost count the drunks stretched out across the surrounding graves. The fresh air begins to clear my mind. I can see my car resting on the fence I must have crashed through last night. I hope the lights are turned off and my battery is charged. If not, I won't be getting out of this very gracefully.

Luckily the car starts. The hell with those idiots lying out there, I'm getting home to clean up. I just might make it to work on time. A hot shower, a cup of instant coffee and toast steady me for the day. Grabbing loose change from an ashtray on my dresser make me think of my wallet. It's nowhere to be found. Crap – it must have fallen out at the cemetery. I will have to wait until this evening to look for it.

The day drags on forever. Then at quitting time the boss said, "Tom, come to the Friday night planning meeting over dinner. It will be steak at the Cow Shack."

"Well sure, I can make it." 'Damn, it will be dark before I'll get out to the cemetery to look for my wallet', I think to myself.

The steak dinner is excellent. I make all kinds of excuses to get out of there early. I thought they would never get done talking about office supplies and days off protocol. The door slams me in the butt as the sun drops over the horizon. The moon appears to be full and there are no clouds. With my luck, I should expect a *Dark and Stormy Night.*

Turning into the cemetery gate, the headlights illuminate the flattened fence for just an instant, then swings over to where I slept last night. Letting the car idle and headlights on, I get out looking for the tombstone that pillowed my head the night before. All the idiots are gone, so I guess everyone lived. My wallet lay open with my driver's license out on the grass. My senses relive that musky scent from last night. My pickled mind cannot mask that smell. Leaning over to pick up my wallet and license intensifies the odor.

I can hear an eerie humming and scraping in the distance. What a crazy thing I am doing, standing in a cemetery with a full moon, listening to the sounds of humming and rocks scraping. All I need now are wolves howling and vampires flapping their bat wings. A cold chill pushes out goose bumps and a cold sweat. I quickly walk back to my car and waste no time getting out of there.

Several hundred yards down the road I see a young woman standing by the roadside. She is wearing a flimsy garment, looks cold and in distress. I stop beside her, roll down the passenger side window, and ask, "Can I be of any assistance to you."

"I'm lost and I want to go home." She said.

"I can take you, where do you live?"

"I don't know. We recently moved here and I cannot remember the address. I don't even know how I got out here. Can you help me?"

"You bet." I said. "What's your name?"

"Valerie. And what may I ask is your name?"

"Tom, you can call me Tom. Well Valerie, you can sleep in my spare bed room tonight, then tomorrow I'm off work and we can find where you live."

"Your place?"

"Yes, you can trust me. I'll even give you the key to the bedroom, if that will make you feel safer."

She opens the door and slides onto the passenger seat. The dash lights illuminate her face. She is beautiful. Her gauzy clothes appear to be night clothing and the lighting shines through to the under garments. I can faintly smell that musty odor and lower the windows.

She clutches her arms around herself as if she is cold. I respond by closing the windows and turning on the heater. Placing her left hand on my forearm, she gazes into my eyes and said, "Tom, I feel safe being with you. Maybe after I have a night's rest I'll remember my address or where I live. I feel tired, lonely and scared." Then she leans her head against my shoulder.

Arriving at my house, I escort Valerie by the arm, to steady her through the front door. She looks around as if to memorize every aspect of the house's interior. "Valerie, would you like something to eat before I show you the bedroom?"

"No, I'll wait until later. I will let you know if I get an appetite.

She follows me up the stairs and to the spare bedroom. I show her the key kept on the bed stand, turn down the bed and fluff the pillow. "Does everything look O.K.? There is an adjoining bathroom through that door." I said, pointing to the bathroom wall.

"If you don't mind, I would like to rest now. You cannot know how much I appreciate what you are doing for me." Then she pulls my head down to kiss me on the cheek. Her lips are cool to the touch. You might even say that they are cold. 'I guess she really was cold in the car.'

I smile and step back. "There may be some suitable bed clothing in the dresser's top drawer. You are welcome to use whatever is there. I am going downstairs to fix myself a drink. You can join me later if you feel up to it."

"I don't think I will join you. Where is your room, just in case I wake up startled, or need something?"

"I'll be down the hallway next to the stairs. I wake easy, so just call out or knock on the door. You shouldn't have any problems here. There are only hoot owls calling or the occasional dog barking. Good night and sleep tight." I walk away, close the door and go downstairs to the kitchen for my drink – a double highball.

Early in the morning, before sunrise, I feel Valerie slip into my bed. 'Maybe she is cold and needs to warm up next to me', I think.' Rolling over to face her, I thought I could feel her staring at me. "Are you cold? Do you need something?"

"Sssshhh. You are what I want and need," followed by a long passionate kiss.

I feel a couple of pinpricks on my lips. I do not remember her wearing braces, and then my mind goes blank as pleasure courses through my body. In the morning Valerie is gone, but there is a note on the pillow. "I remembered where I live, thanks to you. I can go there by myself. I will return tonight to thank you again. You have no idea how much pleasure I had last night. You will be in my dreams all day. Until tonight, Valerie."

The nightly visits continue for a month. I feel energetic but my friends tell me I look pale and should get some sun. After sunset Valerie visits again and we have rough sex all night. In the morning I take a close look at myself in the mirror after a shower. I can barely see the small puncture marks on the side of my neck. I have been asking Valerie where she lives so I could visit. She has been very evasive.

"Close." She had said.

That night she returns again. We slept after our arduous love making, but later I managed to wake, and then pretend to sleep. Just before sunrise, Valerie carefully gets out of bed, and silently goes to the spare bedroom where she puts her bed clothing in the dresser drawer, then leaves the house wearing the same thin garment as the first night I found her. Tracking her at a distance is hard. I cannot use a flashlight without her knowing I was following. Luckily the moon is bright, but not full. I was shocked when she enters the cemetery and goes to the mausoleum. I sit on a nearby tombstone until the sun comes up. There above the mausoleum door is the inscription, "Valerie Valentine, struck down too early in life. May she be with us for eternity." Dumbfounded, I sit for hours in the sunlight. A caretaker stops and asks if I need help.

"No." I said. "I'll be O.K. I just need time to think."

At nightfall I am prepared for her nightly visit. At sunset, candles are lit. A bottle of rich red wine is warmed and placed bedside with crystal glasses. Reinforced restraints are carefully positioned around the bed, hidden from view. I am showered, shaved, cologne applied and ready for action. Valerie appears beside my bed, nude, and bathed in the candlelight.

"You did not have to go through so much work to make me comfortable and your bedroom prepared like this."

"Nothing is too good for you my love. Come to me."

66

After several hours of love making, we rest. "I would like to try something new. I have been reading about bondage sex. Would you like to try it?"

"Yes, anything you want. I trust you and feel safe with you."

"Good. I have everything prepared." Pulling out the restraints, I buckle and cuff Valerie. There is no way she can escape. "Now my love, I know everything about you. I followed you last night back to your mausoleum. I want to be with you forever, but had to take precautions to ensure my safety."

Valerie smiles and looks up at me. "Yes, we will be together forever." With that said, she casually lifts her restrained arms and legs, breaking her bonds with ease to reach out to me.

Later we walk hand-in-hand beneath the moonlight, stopping to enjoy the beauty of the Big Black Swamp. We gaze out over the shimmering water. Insects and creatures serenade us. She feeds on me until I tingle. "We must hurry to our crypt before sunlight." She said.

A wake in the water approaches them unnoticed. A large crocodile lunges out of the water grabbing Tom by his leg pulling him down deep into the murky water. Valerie screams and not seeing Tom surface, jumps into the water, searching to rescue him. Large teeth clamp down on her waist, twisting and thrashing, tearing and shredding, until just small pieces of flesh slowly settle to the bottom of the swamp.

The Louisiana Intelligencer – Two weeks later

The State Police is warning everyone not to fish or go near the Big Black Swamp. There is a large white crocodile preying on people. It is said that it will swim through its victim's blood, apparently swallowing the bloodied water while eating flesh. It has been shot, speared, dynamited and hooked but cannot be killed. Fish and Wildlife experts have tried trapping it, but it is not attracted or interested in fish as bait. It also appears that the crocodile is only seen at night and is attracted to bright lights and the people that hold them.

The Sorcerer

It all started when I woke from a fantasy dream. Swinging out my arm in a horizontal arc while pivoting out of bed, my clothing dressed me. "What. Did I sleep in these?" I thought. My subconscious had apparently selected the clothing I wear, before becoming fully awake and was first now becoming aware of my thoughts.

Rising from bed, my thoughts turn to breakfast. Waffles and bacon come to mind and I am immediately rewarded with tantalizing smells of waffles and bacon, with a fresh coffee aroma that is already sweeping cobwebs out of my brain. "No way. Did my girlfriend Sabrina sneak in to prepare my breakfast?"

Entering the kitchen, I find no one about. Waffles and bacon are set on the table with strong coffee. Everything just the way I like. Even the orange juice tasted freshly squeezed with small bits of pulp floating on top. After finishing the best breakfast I've had since leaving home, I leave the kitchen to fire up my computer and think about the dirty dishes that will have to be washed, dried and put away.

Checking my email and responding to messages that needed to be addressed, my thoughts turn to a second cup of coffee. The pleasant aftertaste from the first cup lingered in my mouth with an addictive draw. Entering the kitchen reveals a spotless view. No dirty dishes to be dealt with. No clean dishes to be put away in the cabinets - just a fresh pot of coffee ready for consumption. "What the hell happened here?" My thoughts return to my dream the previous night. Chants, incantations and a man looking older than dirt mentally prodded my mind. Then there was that vile tasting drink he forced down my throat. The gagging that nearly made me throw up returned to my memory. I now remember the heat my body experienced after swallowing the nasty foul liquid.

In my dream, I really thought my death was imminent. Even my dream had hallucinations. Words also return to my conscious, words of caution, threats and warnings of events to come. "You will remember spells, potions, curses and magic when needed. Your mind will absorb all things from the past, current and the future.

Your memory will be like nothing before, endless in breadth and infinite in time. No problem will be too complicated for you to fathom. You will be my successor to maintain the order of the world. All evil will be yours to combat and overcome. After you have achieved this pinnacle of mental acuity, you will belong to the world and it's destiny.

Your reward for this call to duty will be anything you desire, tangible or not. Be forewarned - a reward conjured that is harmful to others, will render you vulnerable to your enemies, of which there are many. If you ever find yourself overwhelmed by the duties chosen for you, a chant of "Sorcerer Not" repeated three times will remove you from this calling, but you will still be open to retribution by those who wish you harm. Now return to deep sleep while you are fully prepared".

An energetic spring comes to my gait, my mind seems to be sharper and working faster, while my body responds from more muscle tone and reaction. "No, this can't be real." Laughing, "That was just a dream."

Returning my thoughts to that second cup of java, I found my mug is already filled and at the perfect temperature for consumption, but the carafe is already refilled to the full mark. It appears that everything I think becomes reality.

Opening my front door to retrieve the morning newspaper finds me facing a strangely dressed man. Stern facial features tries to intimidate me while a low growl precede a raised arm drawn back to strike. My immediate thought is to block the blow and his strike is blocked. A look of surprise comes over his face. His attention turns to see what has obstructed his swing enabling me to push him backwards and down the landing steps. He is knocked unconscious when his head makes a violent contact with the sidewalk.

After glancing up and down the street to see if the actions were seen, I drag my attacker into the house and secure him to a chair with duct tape. A glass of ice water thrown into his face arouses my attacker. He begins to rapidly mumble in a language that is unknown to me, while the past few minutes flash through my mind. I have questions for him but cannot formulate them into sentences. His eyes gradually focus on me and he starts to speak in English with a heavy accent that I cannot identify.

"You are the current select one. You must reject your gift, or die, to allow another, more entitled one to assume the role as 'The Sorcerer'. I have been foretold of your enlightenment and charged with your corrective action. I must inform you of the dangers that lay ahead if you continue on your current path. Many entities will be employed to achieve your failure or demise. Your days and nights will be a continuous confrontation. There will be no rest for you. You will be living a nightmare".

While not fully understanding my current role, anger boils up at this premature attempt to stomp out what ever I am becoming. "You are not accomplishing what you were sent here for. You do not scare me. I am going to fully realize what has happened to me. After I remove your binding, you can return to your employer and tell him, or her, that you failed."

My attacker leans forward, straining against his restraints, while uttering garbled speech as his body dematerializes. Dusty debris falls past the duct tape, falling to the floor as piles of dirt gathered.

I mentally visualize a dustpan and brush sweeping up the piles of dirt and dropping it into a waste can. Sitting down I began to practice my new found skills before leaving the house to begin my new life.

Sweet Revenge

Barbara always thought she had the perfect marriage. She lived in a million dollar house, her husband Mark, is handsome and earned a very good income with the state. She had a successful business that sold antiques, folk art and crafting supplies.

Lately Mark has been a little distant. She wasn't worried, thinking he was extra busy at work, as he had taken on additional responsibilities and working late nights. Sometimes he worked until the early mornings.

Tonight she is working on the books for her business. The accounting has become tedious as her company grew. Watching over fifteen workers with scheduling and payroll consumed more hours than she liked. Soon she will be able to hire a manager for the store to free up hours for her to enjoy the fruits of what she has built. Maybe even go on a vacation with Mark.

Hearing a car door slam shut she thought, *"Mark is home early tonight."*

Entering her makeshift office, Mark threw down his briefcase and said, "I'll be leaving on a business trip tomorrow, and I'll be gone for a week. I'm going up to get a good night's sleep."

No talk or 'Hello Dear.' He must have had a bad day again. I'll go up and put out his clothes to pack for the trip.

Mark was gone when she woke the next morning. She could still smell his scent on the bed clothing. Inhaling deeply, she again thought how lucky she is to have such a good life with him. Rising and making some breakfast for herself, she heard the front door bell ring. The mail man handed her a large brown envelope, certified delivery, "You have to sign for it lady." After signing the card, he ripped off the card and left.

Smith and Brown, Attorneys At Law was the return address. Curiosity overcame her as she tore open the envelope, thinking that her lawyer was William Barkley.

Opening the triple fold stack of paper, the word 'Divorce' leaped out at her. "This has got to be some mistake. Those idiots have got the wrong woman." Rushing back to her office, she started reading the document. 'Irreconcilable differences' burned into her mind.

Her body went cold as she read. She called her lawyer, Bill, and listened while he comforted her, stating he would contact Mark and talk to him. There had to be some mistake.

The next several weeks passed in a blur. Bill stated, "Mark has no case. I'm sure he will come to his senses and come back to you. He will loose everything he has if he continues with this. Try not to worry, and just continue on like normal until we get this settled."

During the third week, Barbara received word that Bill, her lawyer died from a heart attack. Contacting all her friends for a referral to a good divorce lawyer, their consensus was a John White, a newcomer to town. Contacting John White proved fruitfull as he had very few clients due to his business just being recently opened. Going to his office, she told him everything known to her. "I'll check out all the information and get back to you as soon as possible," he said.

Eight the next morning, John White called. "There is a lot of funny business going on with this case. Did you know that your previous lawyer, Mr. Barkley was actually retained and paid by your husband? This is very unethical for Smith & Brown, Mr. Barkley and your husband. I have also found out that your husband has declared bankruptcy, has no assets, while his outstanding debts exceed his foreseeable future income. In fact, your business has been attached as collateral to cover some of the debts."

"No assets. This house alone is worth over a million dollars and our vacation house, investments, and bank accounts are worth millions. How in the hell can this happen. Mark has always taken care of everything but my store, and I remember see the accounting ledger for the others. This is unbelievable."

"Checking into the money trail, I have discovered that most all the assets are under the name of Deborah Miller. Further checking shows that she is your husband's mistress. I do not have documentation to prove this, but everything leads me to that conclusion."

Fury replaced bewilderment as Barbara quickly regained her senses. Renting a moving truck, she loaded up the most expensive items in her store and hired her most trusted employee, with a car trailer, to load up her husbands restored Jaguar, to follow her to her parents home in Southern Illinois.

Returning to her million dollar mansion, she received another certified envelope stating that the Jaguar had been transferred to the senior partner of Smith and Brown and he wanted to know it's location.

Over the next several months, her Attorney John White had, through his rather thorough investigations, discovered that her husband planned everything to the smallest detail. After the divorce proceedings, the judge became owner of the mansion; Mark received a promotion and married a Deborah Miller. Barbara lost everything.

Eating out one evening, to get away from her parents, Barbara ran into an old friend, Cecilia Young. Cecilia was the Homecoming Queen and winner of many beauty contests. Cecilia went to Hollywood and became a Starlet, who never made big time, but instead became a very high priced hooker. She decided to come home for a vacation of sorts. Sitting at the table, listening to Barbara's story, Cecilia formulated a plan and asked her good friend, "What would you rather have? Revenge or some of the money you lost?"

"Well, there is no way I could legally get any money, so I guess that my answer is Sweet Revenge."

"Leave everything to me Honey, and keep your ears tuned to the gossips. If you need to laugh to sooth your emotional wounds, you'll be recovered one hundred percent, very soon."

Cecilia first found out where Mark hung out after work and where he played on the weekends. She wore the sexiest outfits to attract his attention and gave him the most beguiling pick up lines she knew. Soon she was sleeping with him in her rented apartment outfitted with the best HD video recorders on the market. Every angle and sound was recorded from multi-directional points. Every facial feature and every mole or skin defect was recorded in stereo and HD. It was a truly professional quality pornographic film with Mark as the star. Careful editing rendered Cecilia unidentifiable.

Mailing a beautiful copy of the disk to wife Deborah produced the wanted results. Mark and Deborah was quickly divorced, with Mark loosing everything and Deborah getting alimony forever, or at least until she remarried. The ethics committee deciding that Mark's participation in the porno film was not in line with his state position relieved him from his position.

Deborah, feeling bad about what happened to Barbara, decided to make an anonymous gift of one million dollars to her.

One year later, Barbara, Deborah and Cecilia become close friends.

An irate husband killed Mark because Mark was stalking and harassing a Cecilia look-a-like. The killing was declared self-defense.

Poetic justice does happen once in a while.

X - Rated

"Come on, you can do it. Enjoy it and let your mind go blank. Just pretend you're acting in a movie. Yah, you're a movie star. This is a scene that's crucial to the story. Just go with it."

Melanie started chocking and gagging. She pulled away, spitting out the foamy liquid. Her eyes were tearing up and snorted to clear her nose. Coughing to clear her throat the beer bottle slipped down from her hand. She could never chug beer like Marci who won again. Lifelong best friends, they were called the M & M twins.

Marci aspired to be a movie star. A flair for drama and ambiguous statements always created situations that would get her in trouble. Melanie wiped her mouth and nose with the back of her hand. Lifting her skirt, she wiped away the tears. Looking at Marci, Melanie knew that her friend would make it in Hollywood. She had the looks and scrappy personality needed to succeed. She could memorize the lines from a movie with one viewing. Body language had the clarity of spoken words. A flash of her eyes could stop a charging bull. No bull, she really could.

Beer had dribbled down from the corners of her mouth onto her best blouse. She sniffed at the wet material smelling like an old brew house. Now she had to go home to change before her date with Mike. If her sister smelled the spilt beer, my Mom and the whole town would hear a made up sordid story of what happened. She could make a mountain out of a molehill. Why couldn't the little twit look up and admire me like other pesky younger sisters do.

"Marci! Look at this. Now I have to go home to clean up and change. You're always getting me in trouble. You know Mike doesn't like for me to drink."

"Oh, stop worrying. My house is closer and you can wear one of my blouses. No one is home and no one will know how clumsy you are."

"O.K., but only if you wash it while I clean up and change."

"Done, but we better leave now. Throw the bottles into the bushes and let's get out of here."

Billy, the town bully, is sitting behind the bushes and narrowly escaped being hit by the hurled bottles. He could not see the girls from this vantage point but heard everything. His imagination went wild. "I'll have to follow them to see what else they're up to." He recognized Marci's voice but could not place Melanie's. Waiting a few minutes before standing up, he tried to figure out what guys were with the girls. Too bad the guys didn't speak. Those two girls dated the same guys all the way through school, and he knew that they were not involved in an orgy like that. He'll hang back and follow them back to Marci's house.

Rushing through the front entrance, Marci threw the door shut, and did not notice that it did not latch or lock. Melanie had her blouse off before reaching Marci's bedroom. Luckily, they were the same size. A similar blouse was yanked from the closet and while Melanie checked it before putting it on, Marci put the smelly blouse in the clothes washer.

Billy had walked up to the bedroom window as Melanie stood in her bra checking out the blouse and wondered where the rest of the group was. *"The guys must be in the kitchen drinking,"* he thought. Billy ducked as Marci rushed back into the bedroom.

Melanie put the blouse on and flopped onto the bed and squealed. "Just think, a whole night with Mike and no one to bother us, and my little sister will not be around."

Billy, worried that he would be seen if he raised his head to see what is going on, waited to hear what else developed, and he waited, and waited, and waited.

86

Mission

He stares at me through cold dead eyes, taking in every facet of my face. Turning his head, he glances at the naked woman sprawled out on the bed. Her pose is un-natural and with little modesty. Blonde hair is spread out as though she just came in after being caught in a windstorm. His focus returns to me. I look past his shoulder at the nude woman. She is beautiful with those deep blue eyes, relaxed lips, mouth open as if to speak, and a figure to die for. She would have been more beautiful if not for that small round hole, trickling blood, in the center of her forehead. Yes, she is dead, definitely dead. More so than a dry-docked fish. My gaze returns to the face staring at me. Wondering what is in his mind, I see him raise his right hand and look at the gun he holds, while the smell of cordite fills the air.

I turn away from the mirror to take inventory of my surroundings. The women's black clothes tossed across a chair and expensive shoes under them on the seat. A purse is on the dresser; it's contents dumped out. Pushing around the spewed items with my finger, an intricately printed business card caught my attention. "Black Widow. Assassin For Hire." No photo, phone number or address is shown.

My memory only goes back to pull up the last twenty-four hour block of time. Sometimes there are a few additional little flashes from my past, and they always involve someone murdered, or getting murdered.

"What am I? Who am I?"

I cannot remember where I sleep, or even if I do sleep. Without a past, how could I ever break this cycle of death? Do I eat? I don't remember food - what I like or do not like. Instinctively I begin wiping down everything I could have possibly touched. Stopping to look down at the woman, I wonder about her story. What kind of woman was she? Did she really deserve this? Knowing in my heart that I did this. But why? One last check around the room and I leave. After checking the hallway for traffic, I head for the window and hopefully a fire escape.

I hail a taxi and the driver said, "Where to?"

I don't know what to tell him and stutter, "Take me to a cheap hotel or a restaurant, which ever is closer."

I wake in an apparently cheap hotel room. It's early morning and I have no sense or memory of a past. In a chair sits a man stripped to his waist, tied with an electrical cord. His head is slumped forward. White foam dribbles down his chin. A syringe hangs in his arm. No obvious signs of life. A message is scrawled across his chest with a permanent marker that lies open on the floor in front of the chair. The message reads, "The Future of All Drug Dealers."

I sense that this situation has happened to me before. Questions that seem to have been previously asked come to mind. What am I? Who am I?

Something or someone in my mind speaks – "Mission. Stay on your mission."

"Mission. What the hell is my mission?" A painful ache forms behind my eyes. "Now what?" I think I must be crazy. A strong feeling tells me to get away, but first to sanitize the area. "How do I know this?"

After an area clean up, I stop to view myself in a mirror. I see a tall man, sandy hair with slight curl, ruddy complexion, dressed neatly in a black suit and cold dead eyes. I wince at the monster in my reflection. Yes, I am a monster on a mission.

Exiting the room I walk to an elevator and push the #1 button. When the door opens I walk across the lobby and through the main doors. A cab stops to my raised hand.

"Where to mister?" Asked the cabby.

"How about a cheap restaurant or hotel. Which ever is closer."

Patting my coat, I can feel a wallet. Pulling out the wallet to check on money to pay the cabby, my driver's license flips into view. Matt Maxwell it says. That must be me. Matt Maxwell does not sound like a name that fits me, but that's my photo. The face shown is more compassionate than the image seen in the mirror earlier. The eyes are softer and there is a hint of a smile unlike the mirror's image.

I wake up in a field. Sirens scream in the distance coming toward me. Turning my head I see a woman also on the ground. Her eyes open and she glances around. Confusion spread across her face.

90

Behind her a car is mangled, smoke coming from the engine. A taxi is rolled over on its back like a dead bug, fifty feet away.

Stumbling to my feet I check the woman for injuries. She is not bleeding and there are no apparent broken bones. She moans, "Save my son. He's still in the car." Staggering toward the car I see little fingers of fire starting to encircle the front half. A young child's cry pleads, "Mommy". Yanking the back door open, I release the boy from a booster seat. Like his mother, there is no blood or visibly broken bones. Returning him to his mother, I lean over to place the boy in her arms. They are both crying and the mother talks softly and soothingly while holding him in a tight hug.

Stumbling to the taxi to check on the cabbie and found no pulse. There is a family photo taped to the sun visor of a woman, two small children and the cabbie.

Exhausted, I sit and drunkenly lay back flat on the ground. My bloody hand comes away from a painful spot on my head. The voice in my head comes to me, "Your mission is done. Relax and come home."

A slight grin comes to my lips, my eyes warm and the sun gradually fades from my sight.

Menw's Clothes

My story of enchantment began years ago, more than a lifetime earlier, when my great-grandfather, Menw, which means wizard in the Celtic language, owned a costume warehouse. When he un-expectantly disappeared, I, as his sole living relative inherited everything.

His living quarters were in a small portion of the second floor of the warehouse. There all his personal belongings lay as when he passed away. It was a challenge for me trying to identify or even gain access to the many and strange items. Cleverly locked Chinese chests resisted attempts to open. Unusual, unidentifiable items were found in the most unlikely spaces. A few of the items were labeled, but the hand printing on the labels were not to be identified in any dictionary or reference book. I was in over my head.

Numerous strangers called for appointments to examine the estate for individual purchase. Retaining a lawyer was out of the question due to the lack of money. I was determined to work my way through this problem.

Great-grandfather's office records were complicated, but meticulous, and up to date. The local theatrical group had a revolving contract to outfit their productions and the occasional movie production house filming in the area utilized his wares. Still, the lack of money flow was a hindrance to getting the business back on a profitable basis.

The walk-in traffic was steady and I started to realize a trend. Rentals preceding a full moon were heavier and the customers stranger, or maybe even weirder. Costumes rented just before the full moon were orientated toward horror or mystical and always selected from a grouping kept separate from the main inventory. They also had a distinct, different smell and look about them. They were very old, handmade and the material was hand-woven from a coarse, un-identifiable fiber. These customers were very particular and specific about what they wanted. No substitutions were acceptable like the more flexible common renter. They even seemed agreeable to pay the premium fee attached to this select inventory.

One evening while trying to open a particularly frustrating locked wardrobe, I was drinking a little too much wine and wondered if the select inventory contained a safe cracker's outfit. Unlocking the vault revealed that yes, indeed, there was such a costume. Putting down the glass of wine, I donned the clothing. Looking at myself in the vaults antique full-length mirror, I felt a change in my demeanor. A tingling that quietly turned into a feeling of self-confidence. Picking up my unfinished wine, I returned to the living quarters where I began to unlock all the boxes, containers, wardrobes and chests on the first attempt. Treasures and rare items were revealed to me. I removed some gold coins and relocked everything. The lack of sleep and over indulgence of wine put me to sleep with my head resting on my hands, on the coins, on the desktop.

The morning's light filtering through the window burned through my eyelids to wake me. No, I did not dream last night. There under my forearms lay a small pile of gold coins. Their imprint embossed on my skin and they hurt like hell.

That morning, I visited four different coin shops to get the best appraisal. The amounts was staggering. The dealers all asked the same questions. "Where did you get these coins? Do you have provenance? Are they stolen? Do you have proof of ownership? Let me see your Photo I.D." I deposited the checks into the company's bank account, and then paid off all bills to date.

The remainder of the day was spent looking over all the costumes held in the special vault. I prepared a list of garments that filled me with fear thinking what would happen with their wearing. Others filled me with a curiosity and wonderment of "what if?"

Later that night after closing time and double locking the doors, I donned a period English constables uniform. I was immediately transformed into a dense fog strangled street. It looked like a movie scene of London in the 1800's. A woman came running down the street, throwing the thick fog back like a door opening, with a madman chasing her holding a scalpel high in the air. 'Oh my God. It's Mr. Hyde. He's going to murder that poor woman.' Gathering my senses, I blew the whistle hanging from my uniform.

Ignoring my presence and my whistle, Mr. Hyde caught the frantic woman by her long wafting hair. Yanking her backwards off her feet, the woman's head struck the cobbles of the street with a loud crack. She was trying to scream and yell out for help, but only hoarse guttural sounds managed to escape her mouth. In a fraction of a second the mad man was at her feet tossing the long dress up over her head, partially smothering the pleas for help, holding the scalpel ready to slice.

Coming to my senses, I approached the kneeling man with my raised nightstick in hand, threatening to do bodily harm if he did not stop. He stopped his hand at mid arch, looking at me as if I were the deranged one. With a rolling movement he disappeared into the fog. Removing the dress from the woman's head, I pulled her to her feet as she berated me for the loss of her fare. As her image and irritating voice faded, I reappeared in the warehouse, still in uniform.

Over the next several months I donned other special costumes and experienced many adventures, loves and experiences. Period treasures were taken with me on these time travels to make my presence credible and enjoyable. At no time was my appearance questioned. I was always treated as a very rich and welcomed visitor. Beautiful women threw themselves at me, and men maneuvered to become associated with me. When the adventure concluded, I would always return to my living quarters, on the second floor of the warehouse. The magical costumes were returned to their vault.

As the bottom line of the business grew, I ventured out to make my mark on the world. Strange people stopped me in the streets, talking in languages that I did not understand. Strange facial looks were expressed as I tried to reply and sometimes responding with a finger poke in the chest, or a hand push on the shoulder. Looks of non-comprehension always accompanied the physical response. It almost appeared to me that the time frames of history have become jumbled and the focus of the time scramble is I.

Sitting in my office, I retraced all my activities since assuming my Great Grandfathers role. Nothing I had said or did could have contributed to or caused this apparent confusion of time. I have searched the office and living quarters for any unturned item that might have a bearing on my dilemma. Maybe there is something in the special costume vault that could provide an answer.

Reviewing the costumes for the second time did not reveal any positive results. I then thought of the wardrobe in the living quarters. There were only Menw's clothes. A closer examination brought a set of clothing that resembled those in vault storage. Changing into this outfit produced the fading environment experience before, then as my surrounding details came into focus, I see my Great Granddaddy sitting at a table in his underwear.

"Where in the hell have you been? I was robbed of my clothes and could not return."

"How could thugs rob a wizard to steal his clothes and valuables?"

"Thugs with wizardardly powers. Besides I was incapacitated from drink while entertaining a lovely lass. My mind was not were it should have been. Now, go back and bring me clothes like what you are wearing. And hurry." With a wave of his hand, he faded from view and I reappeared in the living quarters. As quickly as possible I gathered the requested clothing and returned to my near naked charge.

"I thought you were smarter that this. You should have figured out my situation right away. People were laughing at me and refused to bring food, with me penniless and no clothes. I will have a hard time mentoring you when we get back. I still have a business don't I?"

"Well, yes. Your profits are up now, but when you did not return I had to let some of your assets go due to the lack of money flow."

"What assets?"

"Oh, some gold coins and a few trinkets."

"My collection of gold coins. Do you know how much they're worth? It took me years to collect them."

"I'm sorry, but the debt collectors were pounding on the door. What I am worried about now is how to explain your return to the living."

"Nothing to worry about. I rather enjoy this new freedom and a sense of renewed youth. You will continue to run the business under my tutorage and I will expand my search through time for the most unusual and rare treasures for my, or rather our collection.

And now you know how I came about to live this life of enchantment. My Great Grandfather had expanded his adventures further, both the past and future, and our treasures continue to accumulate. Oh yes, did I mention we found the secret of immortality?"

Part Time Wife

As a recent high school graduate, she had zero options. Her stepmother kicked her out of the house and her dad went along with it after listening to all the lies the step-bag told him. She had no money, no job skills and no job offers. Oh, she had offers from the scumbags to live with them or greasy low lifes offering action on the streets. What she did have was exceptional good looks and a body language that turned heads.

Sitting in the café, Veronica took stock of her dismal situation. Two women, sitting nearby, were gossiping about someone they knew. They called the woman *a part time wife* and the idea blossomed in her calculating mind, but she would need a little capital for the clothes and other necessities to pull it off. Yes, a part time wife.

Archie was head over heels infatuated with her and came from a very rich family. He was also a complete loser. Dumb, no street smarts with a 'no love from mother' look, a perfect pigeon to get her stake. Pulling a cell phone from her purse, she checked to see if her dad had cancelled the service. It was still activated. Keying in Archie's number, her heart did a little jump as he answered after the first ring.

"Archie here."

"Archie, this is Veronica and I was wondering if you would like to join me for a drink at the Ninth Street Café?" She could hear the near stutter from excitement as he struggled to reply.

"Sure, when?"

"Well, I'm having coffee now and could use some company."

"I'll be there in ten minutes. Really, just ten minutes so don't leave. O.K."

"I'll be here."

Waiting, a strategy to improve her life grew from a single idea to a master plan.

Archie burst through the door like a fireman to a fire. Frantically looking around, she was spotted instantly, sat and looked at her with puppy eyes. She had already ordered his favorite drink that was sitting in front of him.

"Archie, I need several thousand dollars and don't know where I can get it. Do you having any ideas?"

"What do you need it for?"

"To start my new career. I have been offered a job as a purchasing agent for a large national chain of women's clothing stores, and I need to buy clothes and pay for travel expenses until I receive my first salary checks. After that, per diem and travel allowance will kick in. I should be able to repay the loan in three or four months. Any ideas?"

"Well, sure. I can loan you the money."

"No, I could not ask you for the money. I just knew you would have some idea since you're so good with financial management and smart about business and such."

"Don't be ridiculous. When do you need it? I can write you a check right now."

Veronica suppressed cat eating bird smile. 'Phase one completed', she thought. 'Now to blow this burg and get my life on track.'

After arriving in Chicago, she rented a room in a cheap motel and made a reservation at a five star restaurant. She had blown a good portion of her stake on a classy business suit and after ordering the cheapest salad on the menu, for lunch, put her plan in motion. Almost immediately, a very handsome man wearing an expensive suit stopped and asked if she would like some company. She immediately rejected his offer, 'too polished and experienced' she thought.

The salad was finished and as she lingered over the lemon infused water she was approached by an average looking man who was dressed conservatively, but very expensively, and in his mid thirties. He appeared to be a little shy and asked if he could buy her a drink. "I don't want to appear to be forward, but I could not pass up the opportunity to talk to someone like you. Are you an actress or a model? You look familiar but I cannot place you."

"No, I am a business woman in town for a week before going to New York. I am Veronica and think a little company would be enjoyable. Please join me. I have already had lunch and about to order a drink. Constant travel and living out of a suitcase is a boring life. What is your name and what do you do?"

"My name is Bill and I am a financial advisor. I live in the outskirts of Chi town and also find my time boring and lonesome." After a few drinks, Bill asked Veronica if she was free for dinner followed by a major play. "It's O.K. if you say no, but I thought we could enjoy dinner and entertainment together."

The date went extremely well and they were married at the end of the week. Veronica explained that she was very successful but had to travel constantly throughout the United States and would soon expand internationally. Bill was somewhat disappointed, but being a businessman knew success has a price. Veronica explained that she would return to Chicago one week a month to which Bill was happy knowing that he would have a life that most men could only fantasize about. Within days they had joint bank accounts and she was off to New York, where Veronica repeated what she did in Chicago. Then traveling to San Francisco she married an almost identical man as her first two husbands.

Arriving in Dallas, Veronica set out to fill in and complete her monthly schedule. She found an easy mark in an older lonely oilman. She felt her chosen life was complete, spending one week a month with each of her four husbands. She did not love any of her husbands and considered them a necessary function of her career, something to struggle through to achieve success.

After two years of working through the weekly *honeymoons* Veronica stopped in St. Louis for a vacation away from her four amorous husbands. At the age of twenty, she was at the peak of her career. Lounging poolside at an exclusive hotel she avoided contact with anyone. After constant marital obligations, she just wanted solitude to re-energize mind, body and soul. The wear and tear on her was beginning to take its toll.

A shadow crossed her closed eyes and a spray of water splashed across her face. Irritation opened her eyes as a deep voice apologized for the intrusion. A tall handsome man was standing before her, whipping his hair from side to side. The sun situated directly behind his head haloed his hair. A shiver coursed though her body like an artic chill. She had never reacted to a man like this before. He stood taking in her physical features like he had never seen a woman in a bikini before. She felt extremely self-conscious and giddy like a girl experiencing her first love. He spoke smoothly as he apologized again while she stuttered and stammered trying to answer him.

"Let me buy you dinner to repay you for my clumsy action. I was just shaking the water out of my hair. I had no idea it would fly out on you."

The tingling and itch overloaded her mind as she accepted. "I can't get involved with this guy, it would screw everything up," she thought. Her heart won out over logical thought. "An overnight, successful businessman and on his first vacation," he said. There were no living relatives and he was always too busy to become emotionally involved – before now.

Falling completely in love, Veronica had to re-evaluate her career. She explained to Carlin that she was independently wealthy, inheriting her fortune after her parents were killed in a plane crash. Carlin doted on her, catering to her every need and desire, proposing during the seventh day of their affair.

"Since you have all that wealth, why don't we have pre-nuptials drawn up, just to protect your inheritance?" Suggested Carlin.

"No, my love, everything I have is yours."

They married the next weekend and left on a honeymoon cruise to the Bahamas, on a private yacht, courtesy of joint bank accounts – now empty. New bank accounts were established, and unknown to Veronica, in Carlin's name only.

On a beautiful morning, after an evening of passionate lovemaking, Carlin called for Veronica to come up on deck for a breakfast he had lovingly prepared for her. Fresh fruit and champagne were served. Veronica became very sleepy and nodded off. Carlin watched his wife with a satisfied and happy smile. Opening the bait box, he starts throwing chum overboard while the yacht was dead in the water. Sharks began circling, and they too, enjoyed their breakfast when Veronica was slid over the side. They also enjoyed the fruit and champagne previously served and consumed.

Carlin made a distress radio transmission reporting the 'accident' and started polishing his statement to the officials and the insurance company. They had taken out a five million dollar insurance policy on each other.

The Good And Bad

Whomph. Whomph. Whomph.

The man is lost in the darkened woods, running for his life. Something in the sky is pursuing him. Looking over his right shoulder he sees giant wings coming closer. The thing, whatever it is, started following him, just before dusk. Running and evading the flying creature for the last three hours has left him weak, hungry and thirsty. Instinct tells him he will be dead if he stops or tries to hide. The wings beating the air are becoming louder, and closer. The thing starts to dive, picking up speed. He forces himself to try running faster. The wings quietly slice through the air as it slowly descends upon him, like an owl in the wild, striking prey. A spur pushes out from the wing tip joint. A quick slash brings the man to ground. The thing, a human form with large wings, settles down to stand on its prey. Talons are where toes exist on humans, but this is not human.

The talons tear into the man's back, crushing his spine. He screams in agony as bone is yanked from his body. Then with talons locked into his shoulders, is lifted high into the sky. Moments later the man is dropped from one hundred feet onto an outcropping of rock. Bones are shattered. Regaining consciousness, the man has no feeling from his waist down. His arms are broken, and head concussed. He cannot move his head, but can rotate his eyes. He can see human bones scattered across the outcropping. They gleam in the moonlight. They are gnawed and crushed. He does not know how long he was unconscious and is fearful of the next few minutes. Something that he cannot see begins chewing on his feet and legs. There is no pain, but he can sense pulling and the tearing of flesh. He hears rustling as something approaches him from behind and he feels painful chewing on his ear. A furry animal, a rat, scurries across his head to begin eating his nose and lips. He squeezes his eyes shut hard, as if to force out the pain. Opening his eyes when he feels a larger furry animal brush past his face, he sees and smells a stinking possum looking back and forth, as if checking for competition to the newfound meal. His mind reels in terror as the possum begins chewing just above his groin. The possum enters his stomach and eats half way up to his throat before the relief of death overcomes him. His last thoughts were regret for killing the picnicking couple in the late afternoon.

His soul, a black oily substance, slowly begins the long painful trip down, through the earth's crust, toward the burning core, where other like souls reside. Some will be vomited up through volcanoes for a teasing, temporary exposure to sunlight, only to be thrown back down for another painful re-passing into the earth's core, surely a punishment for their choice of living existence. Others will be forced up through the ocean bottoms, like hell's defecation, to mix with the slime of the sea life's excretion, before passing again, down to the earth's core.

He had no way of knowing that the larger carnivores of the woodland visited him to eat during the night. Come sunrise, the birds of the forest complete their task of cleansing their environment. The partial skeleton, of mostly crushed and eaten bones, remains bleaching in the bright warm sun.

At next dusk, the winged humanoid begins its nightly patrol. A quiet whimper is heard. Dropping down to the tree top level, eagle like vision detects a small being, not much more than a toddler. Lost, scared and quietly sobbing, he does not know where to go or what to do after his parents were viciously killed the day before. The winged humanoid slowly circles, like a vulture descending to its meal, until landing in front of the small boy. Cooing to relax and comfort, it wraps its wings around the boy with caresses that feel like cascading goose down. Cradling the small human in its arms, the creature takes flight into the night.

Risking detection, it flies over the small town, landing at the side door of a church. Mentally voiding the memories of the small child, he sits him on the step and knocks loudly on the door, interrupting the evening service. A quick take off has it out of sight before the door opens. "My heavens, who are you? Where are you from?" exclaims the usher. Looking around and seeing nothing out of the ordinary, the man picks up the child to return to the warmth of the church interior.

The humanoid watched from hidden safety until assuring himself the child was safe, then again took flight, searching, always searching, for the good and bad, exacting punishment and reward to each it's due. The Angel is always on patrol.

A Grave Too Deep

(Previous published in "A Dark And Stormy Night")

Dark ominous clouds boiled overhead, obscuring the grey cast moon, heavy with electricity and threatening a torrential downpour. The air was crisp and bone chilling. The wind screamed through the pines like an Irish Banshee, forewarning the gravedigger, Dugley Deep, of a pending horror. Digging at the bottom of an unfinished grave changed the way sounds were heard. Down there, the wind driven and thrashing pine limbs produced a moaning sound. Dugley, ever diligent of his surroundings, was wary of an ominous presence he felt was shared with the cemetery.

A clawing scratch came from Dugley's spade as he thrust the steel blade, polished from digging many graves, forcibly down through the hard unbroken gritty soil. He was far from finished with his task at hand. Needing the necessary depth of six feet six inches, the last measurement was only four foot and five inches. Only his head was above ground level. If one could view the rotating head, observing his surroundings, it could be thought a bodiless head was spinning around in a possessed manner. A headless corpse being sought by his lost center of control, you might say.

Broken ground flew up from the hole, landing in a heap to be used as back fill after the coffin was lowered, and the vault lid sealed, onto a concrete box. A ladder was positioned at one end of the deepening rectangular hole, an escape route, up the ladder and through the maze of mostly upright stones, to arrive at his vehicle, in the least amount of time. His rusty old pickup was in dire need of a tune up. The tires were near bald that prevented driving up close, on the damp grass. To try a speedy escape would fail and just result in spinning tires on the slippery vegetation, and capture in what surely would be a horror scene.

He thought he could hear someone calling out his name. Dugley stopped digging to focus his hearing. A quick look around did not relieve his apprehension. A shiver coursed through his body as he sidled up to the mantel lantern,

114

comforted by its warming glow. The lantern was battling the heavy darkness closing in, and seemed to be loosing. Picking it up, he gently shook the light and smiled reassuringly, hearing the fuel slosh. Anxious to finish his job, a quick measure of depth proved disappointing. It was only five feet deep. It will take another one and one half more to dig, before he could go home. *The deeper you get, the harder the digging*, he thought.

A coyote howled in the distance, answered by a nearby barking dog. Murmuring surrounded Dugley, forcing another check of his surroundings. A mist fell onto his face. Looking up he saw a large opening in the cloud cover directly above. There were no night birds flying. No tree limbs to hide creatures of the night or to obscure his view of the sky. *Where did that moisture come from?*

Dugley trembled, remembering stories told of people recording voices from the cemetery graves. Some recordings were made during séances to locate important papers, treasures or identities of a spirit's murderer. Other stories revolved around 'dousers' identifying unmarked grave occupants and their gender. Dugley did not believe in superstition, but always avoided tempting the spirits. He did not walk on occupied graves and always spoke in a reverent voice when working at the cemetery.

The spade struck something metallic in the ground. '*How can that be?*' he thought. This is undisturbed ground. More chills coursed through his body, and a brain freeze weakened his thinking, as he methodically dug around the struck object. Sparks flew as the spade inadvertently struck the object again. Prying the metal up with the spade brought an ancient looking sword to the surface of the grave floor. A purple aura surrounded it. A shiny surface reflected the lantern light and there was no oxidation of the metal or deterioration of the handle's rough finish.

Dugley knew from his readings, that sharkskin was used for making sword handles because the sand paper like surface would secure the sword in a man's hand, made slippery with blood during combat. But sharkskin, no matter how tanned or preserved, would not stand up to this apparent time period. Picking up the sword produced a rather unpleasant tingling up his arm and across his chest, stopping at his heart. A heated flush flowed over his body, then changed to a deep chill.

He heard crying, but there was no one there. Looking around he noticed a marble angel, part of a headstone, three graves down, tears making dark lines running down from her eyes. His body tried to continue in its mechanical chore of digging, when the ground gave way to a subterranean opening. Dugley landed on all fours, disoriented and in pain from the fall.

Looking up through the grave opening made the hole look small. He could not estimate the distance due to the lack of light. The lantern did not penetrate this deep and appeared but a glow.

A singing came from what appeared to be a long tunnel, not high enough to allow upright walking but maneuverable if kept hunched over. Feeling his way along the shallow tunnel Dugley approached a lit cavern with no evidence of a light source. It seemed the air just glowed. Small gnome like people were cavorting in what appeared to be a tavern of sorts. Scantily clothed maidens teased and flirted while serving mugs of beer to groups of little wrinkled aged men.

The servers did not rebuff attention from the little men, but were laughing and giggling as they banged the large drafts on the roughly made tables. The small men were dressed in dark brown and bright green clothing. Their faces were deeply etched. Their eyes sparkled with delight and all had heavy beards. Their skin tone was dark, belying their existence underground. Cautiously inching forward and carrying the heavy sword like a cane, Dugley entered the cavern. A shout from the boisterous group caused the merriment to stop. A rush of red nosed, bearded miniature people surged in his direction, as he held up the sword in a defensive gesture.

As the moving sword sparkled in the light, the wee men and servers stopped and kneeled down in front of him with bowed heads and acknowledged his presence in words he did not understand. Lowering the sword, Dugley stared at the blade and noticed inscriptions, in a strange script, on the blade that he previously could not see.

An older, frail looking man stood and slowly approached Dugley, his hands raised in a peaceful gesture, then carefully studied the sword and him with non-threatening expression. Reaching a distance of roughly his height, he began to speak in a voice Dugley understood. "Who are you? How did you acquire our Sword of Wrath? Where did you get it? How did you get here?"

The apparent leader of the group was still mouthing words when Dugley interrupted him. "I was digging a grave, above, when I found this sword buried and then fell through into the tunnel behind me. Please tell me that this is all a dream."

"What is your name?"

"Dugley Deep".

"Dugley Deep. This is no dream. We are the Igennouts that fight the Denizens of the Underground."

"Denizens of the Underground? Who are they?"

"They are the soul suckers of those buried above. We can hold them off, but only the Sword of Wrath can kill them. Many centuries ago they stole the sword, but could not destroy it. They hid it from us thinking they could maneuver around our defenses. Ancient legends tell of the sword's return. Now, please give it to me."

"How do I know that what you are telling me is the truth?" The heated flush left Dugley. A feeling of purpose and honor overcame him. A hissing, clicking and scratching sound echoed, ever louder, through the tunnel behind him. The small people ran back in fear, and started setting up a barricade across the cavern entrance.

"The sword. The sword. Use the sword. It's the only thing that can kill them. Quick, turn around and strike them down."

Turning Dugley could now see in the darkness with clarity. Huge spiders, with blood red eyes and grinding mandibles, filled the tunnel. Swinging the sword struck down the nearest spider and was quickly replaced by another. Raging combat continued for hours without help from the tunnel dwellers behind their barricade. When the last spider was cut down a roar of acclaim echoed through the tunnel. "Now everyone is safe," said Dugley.

"No. That was just a small patrol trying to locate us. Now do you believe we are the true owners of the sword?"

"Yes. Here take the sword." Handing over his found treasure, Dugley's world turned dark.

Dugley woke with a knot on his head. The adjacent grave had given way and the coffin lay in pieces around him. The skeleton lay across him. The fallen ground had nearly covered him and he gripped a long pointed root in his hand.

Along Came A Spider

I had just started eating a freshly grilled burger, cooked rare, on my new patio grill. It was spring and I was enjoying the bouquet of my burger, wafting on a gentle breeze that filtered through the wooded land.

I noticed a large black spider, about four inches in diameter, watching me from beneath the chair next to where I was sitting. It seemed to be moving up and down in a pushup manner. Curious, I tore off a small piece of meat from my sandwich and dropped just in front of her. She made motions like she smelled the tidbit, and then backed away. Fussy eater I thought. Paying more attention to the doneness of the meat, I selected a small portion from a more rare section. Blood oozed from the piece as I pinched it off the patty. Dropping the bloody morsel less than inch in front of her produced a vicious attack leap that resembled a cat on a mouse. After consuming the small bit of meat she looked up at me as if she were thanking me.

Every afternoon through the summer months, unless it was raining, I would eat my lunch on the patio and to feed my new pet spider. I named her Kim, and she would wait for me every afternoon, waiting for her meal. Sometimes she approach and massage my shoe with her two front legs. There were never aggressive moves, just gentle motion and sometimes that little push up bobbing.

Through the fall months Kim became friendlier sitting on my knee then gradually up to the top of the table where she would eat in a mannerly fashion. Late fall the weather became cooler and I noticed Kim was becoming lethargic, moving slower to ascend to the top of the table. I held a clean napkin in my hand to warm it and placed it beside her. She immediately crawled to the center of the napkin and stayed there while I slid it off the table and onto my flat hand and carried her into the house.

I prepared a small box with a couple of pulled and shredded cotton balls. She immediately took to her new home, combing the cotton into a funnel cell. I placed a small plastic sheet on a kitchen shelf and Kim's home on top. Every afternoon she would come out of her box when I placed food there for her. After the first week, I thought that there was something wrong with her, as she would not always eat. Then I realized that I rarely see insects in the house anymore. We were experiencing a mutually beneficial partnership. We're a team.

Sometimes, before she would eat my offered food, she would dance, or perform acrobatics, doing somersaults in the air, or walking on just two legs. She appeared to be happy to entertain me. Maybe she thought this was a kind of payment for my kindness to her.

On a cold, snowy, early February evening, there was a knock on my door. A man stood in the weather, wet and looking miserable. "My car slid into the road ditch. Can I use your phone to call a wrecker?

"Sure. Come in and get warm. How about a cup of coffee or tea?"

"A cup of coffee would be nice. Are you all alone here? Where is your wife?" he said.

Laughing "No, I'm single. It's just me and my pet." I said.

"Oh you have a dog?"

"No, nothing like that. My phone is over there on the end table. Call a wrecker while I get your coffee."

The stranger walked toward the telephone and the easy chair next to it, while I turned to get his coffee from the kitchen. While pouring the coffee I noticed Kim was not in her little house. Probably out hunting insects, I thought. I called out to the stranger, "Do you take cream or sugar."

"No, just black, thank you."

I was returning to the living room, watching the coffee in the cup, trying not to spill it into the saucer when the stranger said something I did not understand. Walking through the entranceway I said, "I'm sorry, I did not hear what you said." There was a little laugh from the stranger standing at my side with my fireplace poker raised over his head in a menacing stance.

The strike to my head knocked me to the floor. The blow brought pain to my head and tears to my eyes. Little stars circled me, just like in the cartoons. I moaned, but could not raise my arm to touch where he hit me. "I want all your money and valuables. Where are they?"

"My wallet is on the kitchen table, take what you want. There is nothing else in the house." The stranger did not like

124

my response and struck me two more times in the head. I thought that I should feign unconsciousness, and then maybe he'll just rob me and leave. I could hear him rummaging through my bedroom, then the kitchen. I heard his satisfied grunt when he emptied my wallet. I had just withdrawn the money from the bank. I always took out the amount that I would need to get through the month.

My head was facing away from the door, but I heard the refrigerator door open and a sandwich being prepared, a bottle of beer fizzed as it was uncapped and poured into a glass. I was getting stiff and sore from laying still so long, but I knew if I moved, he would hear and beat me more. I was at a disadvantage not being able to see what was he was doing.

I heard the smacking from the sandwich being eaten with his open mouth, the gulping from the beer guzzling and a final belch. Now he's going to leave, I thought. Heavy footsteps came back into the living room and then the couch springs protested from a weight dropping onto it. He must have thought he killed me and he's going to take a nap before he leaves. A motioned got my attention. Kim was coming close to a small pool of blood from the gashes in my head. I watched as she made her little push up motions while tasting my blood. She quickly disappeared up the wall and out of my sight. Later, I could hear the heavy breathing from the stranger and thinking he was asleep I tried to move. My arms and legs were numb. I could rock just a little, but not really move. Kim returned and drank more blood. She made trips all night while I lay paralyzed on the floor. During the night the stranger's heavy breathing turned to snores, while Kim went back and forth. Early in the morning as I saw light spilling through the windows and the stranger's snores turned to muffled words and screams. The pool of blood was mostly sucked up and then the stranger was quiet.

My strength was returning and I was able to rock back and forth until I was able to roll over. Feeling was returning to my body but I was still too weak to get up. When the morning light filled the room I saw a terrifying scene. The stranger lay silent, completely encased in a spider web and Kim on his cheek eating him. It took another two hours before I was able to achieve a kneeling position and another hour for me to reach the phone and call 911. By then Kim was gorged from her prey and back in her house sleeping. I removed the web from the stranger's body and finally wiped it from my hands and into the trash when the EMTs and police arrived.

I explained what had taken place, but omitting Kim's participation, and stating rats must have attacked the stranger while he slept. I was worried when the EMTs and police noticed the sticky web residue all over the body. "Doc has to do an autopsy to find the actual cause of death." I did not want to go to the hospital and the EMT patched up my head cuts, telling me to see a doctor, as soon as possible.

Two months later, my neighbor Patsy came to visit. She is a widow, but has always been sweet on me. We were sitting on the couch while she was trying to invite herself to stay overnight. Her arm was around my neck and she came in for a kiss. Kim suddenly fell from the ceiling onto Patsy's head, her legs moving like a blender. Patsy jumped up screaming and swatting her head. Kim was knocked to the floor when Patsy slammed her foot down. The loud squish sounded like cherry tomatoes being stomped. I did not have the heart to tell Patsy that Kim was my house pet and protector. A few minutes later, after a wild Patsy was calmed down, I performed a rather touching burial at sea in the downstairs toilet.

I think that my next pet will be a dog.

Feeding The Monster

I have a monster that resides in his dwelling 100 feet west of my house that needs daily feeding during the cold months. If I neglect caring for him, I suffer a cruel, cold punishment. Daily feedings are a must and cleaning his abode is required semi-monthly to bi-monthly, depending on his daily food intake. Again, if he is not cared for, my punishment is swift and chilling.

My monster has been under my care for about twenty years. I must harvest his food regardless of the weather or my own personal safety or needs, be it medical or maintenance. I must carefully adjust his diet to a narrow quantity and quality. If the food is not nutritional for him, I must increase the quantity to satisfy his needs. If I exceed his nutritional needs, his lair requires a more intensive maintenance schedule.

At first, establishing a maintenance routine mandated an exercise of trial and error. During this period of effort neither of us experienced satisfaction. I still do not know who trained whom for that perfect balance. He can be like a fire breathing dragon, engulfing me in smoke and singed hair. Other times, when he is happy and content, he wraps me in his loving warmth.

The work of caring for him has the side benefit of maintaining my muscle tone and the strenuous cardio effect keeps me healthy from the exercise. My feline friends accompany me when I care for him. I feel they think they are protecting me as they watch, ready to pounce with warnings of hissing and snarls and with deadly swipes of their claws. They do not understand his food and test it with sniffs and occasional nips.

His longevity far exceeds theirs, so they will never experience life without him. In fact, he may outlive me if someone assumes my willing chores when I pass on. I wonder if he will realize what is happening as he slowly dies, after my term of laborious support stops.

Snow, blowing artic winds or torrential rains cannot delay his feedings. If I arrange for a substitute to take over my chores, proper training on the required protocols are a necessity to avoid dangerous repercussions that could endanger my neighbors or anyone else that would be close by. Many visitors are enthralled, or amazed, by his activities and shocked at the effort needed to sufficiently keep him alive. Many are jealous of his benefits, but glad he is not theirs to support and maintain.

Maybe someday I will just rely on my back-up LP furnace and drain the water out of my monster, a wood fired boiler that heats my house. Until then, my demanding and possibly dangerous association with the wood eating monster, must continue with all due caution.

The Clause Syndrome

December 20th.

"Doctor Wagner, I don't think he is going to make it with his rapid aging. His hair and beard have turned snow white. What could be doing this?"

"I don't know Nurse Carron. I've never seen anything like this before. When was he admitted?"

"A week ago, in a coma, and he was a relatively young looking man. Since then he has gained at least 80 pounds. How can that be possible?"

"I have no idea. I have contacted every expert known in the field, and no one knows anything. Not even an educated guess. It's baffling to everyone.

A giant of a man lay in the hospital bed. Tubes are in his nose. IVs are connected to his veins. He is motionless, not responding to sounds or stimulus. A peaceful aura surrounds him and his breathing is slow but steady. Doctor Richard Wagner nods to Nurse Carron to follow him into the hallway.

Images, somewhat like an air traffic controller's screen flows through the giant man's brain. He normally found a secure place to rejuvenate at winter's start, but this year he was found by some do-gooders looking for homeless people, before the conversion was complete. Now his mind is filling in all the blank spaces, completing the total operation. Oblivious to the activity around him, his subconscious continues firming up the logistics required for this year's mission.

December 21st.

The snow is accumulating and the drifts are rising to record heights. Medical specialists scurry to cluster around the comatose man who appears to be sleeping. His skin is ruddy when it should be pasty for a man in his condition. All the electronic monitoring devices show a high level of brain activity and eyes show high REM, rapid eye movement, as if dreaming. Printouts are closely studied and discussed with consultants. Everyone would like this medical emergency to resolve itself before Christmas. They all would like to be home with their loved ones. Hope is holding out for this nameless mystery man. Prayers are said asking for a miracle. Everyone is praying, everyone but John Smith, the man lying in the bed. He has a lot of work to do and cannot take time to respond to those in attendance to his apparent needs.

December 22nd.

The snow is now three feet deep. The city street department is barely keeping up with the street plowing without calling in emergency personnel. Nearby Scott Air Force Base has authorized the use of base personnel and equipment, if requested by the mayor.

Kat Perry, the top neurologist in the area, has been consulted and is on her way to the hospital. She grumbles that she should be flying to Hillsboro to be with her family and is sure someone dropped the ball, missing something basic that would lead to a correct diagnosis. 'I hope they still have that bottle of Tequila to loosen me up, or else I will have to fall back on some of Chuck's Elixir. My muscles really get tense from driving in this damn snow,' she thought to herself. Kat pulls into the staff parking lot and hesitates before loading up a large carrying bag with comfort food for the duration.

December 23rd.

Nurse Nicole Dormeier is manning the nurses' station on the second floor of the St. Joseph Hospital in Highland. The nursing staff is frustrated because of the sporadic problems with the electronic monitors. "Everything seems to go to hell when we are on duty. Why can't everything work the way it is suppose to? It must be payback for what I do after work."

CNA Andrea Doetzel opens the door to Ronald Denoon's room with a bedpan in her cart. Helping patients with their special bowel needs is the most distasteful part of her job. 'I think being a mortician's helper would be a step above this,' she thought. Ronald always looks forward to Andrea's presence and dreams about her hands on him. He greets her with a large and genuine smile.

Sam Rak is visiting her boyfriend Sutton in the room across the hall from the mystery man, as he has come to be called. She is watching him sleep and wondering why he had

136

lost control and crashed his homebuilt glider into Dale Hamil's outhouse. The small building was totally demolished and the EMTs had a terrible time extracting Sutton from the horrible smelling pit beneath the building. Dale Hamil's neighbors are all worried and apprehensive about where and what he is now using since his outhouse is destroyed. Feeling a sudden excitement come over Sam like a summer breeze, she reaches out and touches Sutton's hand. "Nope! That's not it," she murmurs. Still the intoxicating feeling stays with her. 'Something important is coming,' she thinks.

JoAnn Bockenfeld is shopping in the gift shop. She needs some balloons, or some other gift, for her friend who had just delivered identical triplet girls. "Maybe I should just get her some valium, or a gallon of vodka, for when she thinks about their future teenage years – no, that wouldn't be right. I'll get her a year's subscription to that latest computer dating service. That will be something she can really use for the rest of her life, if she uses it the right way."

Jeanette Hammel, the friendly neighbor of the new mother enters the gift shop, looking for JoAnn. "Do you know who the father is? I need to find out and I think you know who it is. It's not that no good manure handler from south of Highland is it? Tell me."

"I don't know. Ask Gary Adolph. He might know who it is, since he comes past that part of town on his way into Highland."

"If you don't tell me, I'll have to ask Burnell Petry, you know, The Wanderer. He knows everything. He has a wider ring of spies than the CIA. If he doesn't know, I'll make him find out. That biological sperm donor can't get away from me." Said Jeanette, who suddenly gets distracted by a baby doll. Jo Ann rolls her eyes, then seeing an opportunity, sneaks out the door, relieved she got away.

Sandra Kohlbrecher stops JoAnn by the elevator. "JoAnn, I am writing a true love mystery novel about the guy who is getting all these women in town pregnant. I need your input to make the novel credible. How about sitting down with me in the visitors lounge and answer a few questions? You know, like who it is and how he feels about all the kids that will be running around with his last name."

"How the hell do you think I know who it is? She just smiles dreamily and says I wouldn't believe her, even if she told me. She is one of my best friends and I feel like a dunce because I don't know a thing about her situation."

"Just come on. Talking about it may just jog something in your memory."

December 24th.

Nurse Carron just finished taking the mystery man's vitals. She pauses before leaving the room, glancing back at the peaceful looking man. "Such a waste, a fine looking man like that. What could possibly be wrong with him? I bet some wonderful woman is waiting at home, anxiously waiting for word of him." Then turning away softly closes the door behind her.

Sneaky John Smith is waiting for the lingering nurse to leave. Quickly he sits up and frees himself of all the tubes and electronic hookups. Stretching, he felt strength returning to his muscles after his long rejuvenation. "Every year the same sequence, for the past two thousand years. What the hell happened this year?" None of his clothes in the closet fit since gaining all the weight. Ripping one of bed sheets into a semblance of an orderly's uniform, he eases himself into and down the corridor stopping at the doctor's lounge. He selectively outfits himself from what is available and makes his way to the street where he instinctively heads for a reindeer ranch at the edge of town. It always amazes him that no matter where he finds the reindeer, they always know him and it seems that every reindeer source has a sled.

Doctor Richard Wagner returns to the doctor's lounge to find someone ripped off his clothes. "What the Hell! Where is security when you really need them? It's not just anyone who is able to wear my clothes." Sitting down, he calls 911 to report the theft. "Maybe it was some drug addict needing money for a buy, or, that new Doctor Frank Tejada, who is trying to take over my patients. Yeah, maybe it's him. I'll sic the cops in his direction. Two can play that game."

It is now 8 p.m. Christmas Eve. Finding the reindeer willing and eager for a romp in the snow, Smith, somehow now dressed as Santa Clause, hitches up his steeds. It is snowing so hard now that visibility is down to a few feet. Pulling up to the loading dock at Walmart, the workers think the reindeer and sled is a promotional event and quickly loads the sled with goodies from a waiting delivery semi.

Every Christmas, it is a different town, and a different experience. Every Christmas, it is different people with different names. Smith wonders where and who he will be next year, but for now he had work to do, and joy to spread. Oh yes, he will have to put the impregnating guy on his naughty list.

140

The Perfect Vacation

The Ad.

The ad stated: Have your next vacation at the Perfect Vacation Dude Ranch. Tell us your fantasy and we will make it happen. Visit our web site to plan your perfect vacation. Dude Ranch – Live the life of the western cowboy on a fully functioning ranch. Hunting Party – Go hunting for elk, deer or buffalo. Guides take out small groups and can guarantee a successful hunt. Hunting party grub is provided. Golf – Play on a world-class golf course where pros are readily available for one-on-one instruction. Mountain Climbing – Learn the techniques that the professionals use. Leisure – Take part in our relaxing

141

sandy beach bordering a 250-acre lake, or use the wide array of watercraft. Scuba Diving - Dive on an authentic ghost gold town. Swim - Do laps or competitive swimming in an Olympic size swimming pool. Role Play – Act out your favorite character from legendary movies. Live the life of your idol movie stars. Once again, you name your fantasy and we will make it happen. All activities are held in the strictest confidentiality.

Mavis looks up from the magazine article. "Mark. Come look at this. We should take a vacation and this looks perfect. We've been complaining about our life being in a rut. This would really spark our lives."

"Let me see." Said Mark as he walked in from the shower.

"Mark, you're dripping water all over the place. Dry off and put on your robe before leaving the bathroom. You're always making a mess."

"Just thought I should put a little thrill in your morning. I have the whole day off so we can enjoy ourselves."

"Get real. Really, what do you think about this ad? We deserve a little adventure and excitement for our third anniversary."

142

Reading the ad brings a smile to Mark's face. "Let's do it."

The Dude Ranch

Flying in is the only way to the Ranch. The flight was smooth and well catered. Landing, the group of vacationers leaves the plane and is directed to board a waiting bus. When they pull up to the main Ranch House, Mavis said, "Mark, this is beautiful. What do you think about it?"

"I'll know more about what I think after we look around."

"Howdy folks. Welcome to Perfect Vacation Dude Ranch. The valets will bring your gear in while you register and then plan out your vacation. Don't be shy about your fantasies. Selections are kept secret from your partners. Keeps everything spicier when you compare notes after the vacation. That will be the time for more role-playing. You can also team up with another couple for a more satisfying adventure." Said Tex, Head Ranch Hand, according to his nametag. "Mr. Mark Smith, why don't you start by registering yourselves, while your wife Mavis starts planning her fantasy with our counselor? You can plan your adventure with the next available counselor when you're done."

"Be glad to, Tex."

Looking back at Mavis from the Registration Desk, Mark can see she is totally focused in designing her fantasy with a female counselor. *'She is most likely setting up reservations for the beach to sun herself and a couple of spa treatments. She is unable to plan anything original.'* He thought.

The First Fantasy

"I want to play the role of a Bond Girl and can I pick the man to act out 007? I need a real man." Said Mavis.

"Anything you want dear. Here is the catalog of available men you can select from. Some of the men available work as ranch hands here and the others are guests that want the same adventure as you. Now you know this is a 48 hour event."

"What do you mean?"

"Well dear, you will be 007's companion, day and night, and that includes enjoying him in bed. You'll really love this fantasy. I have had three of these movie role adventures since I started working here and I have never experienced a dud in a partner yet."

"Will my husband find out?"

"Never, not unless you tell him."

Mavis giggled. "Let's do it." Pointing to a stud pictured on the page, she said, "This guy Jack is the one I want. Where do I sign?"

"A really excellent choice. I'll have to remember him for my next adventure. Ms. Smith, your adventure will start tonight at 9 p.m. and you should report to wardrobe at 8:30 p.m."

"Now remember, you and your husband will be going on the elk hunt the day after your first fantasy."

The Second Fantasy

Mark has finished registering Mavis and himself, then turning around see her sitting in a lounge area on the opposite side of the great room, apparently done with her counselor and waiting for him to finish.

Mark noticed that the next available counselor is male. Sitting down he said, "Well where do we start with this planning?"

"Here is a list our standard fantasies. You can pick from here or we can develop a custom event. We should start with the standard list first."

Scrolling down the list Mark stops on 'Clark Gable and Marilyn Monroe.' "What does this all entail, and who plays the part of Marilyn Monroe?"

"Here is a catalog of women available to play her part. Now I have to tell you that this is a 48-hour adventure and you can also design your own script. You can do and have her do anything you want, as long as no one is hurt in any way."

"Wow. For forty-eight hours? Is it possible that my wife could find out?"

"Nope. Everything done here at the ranch is 100% confidential. The only way she would learn about anything you do is if you tell her. Some of the girls in our catalog work here on the ranch and some are guests looking for the same type of experience as you. Do you see someone in the catalog you like? Choose carefully. You might as well get your money's worth, picking exactly what you want."

"This is unbelievable. This gal Jill, with the great bod, if she is as good as she looks here, you'll see me back here every year."

"A very good selection, Mr. Smith. Your adventure will begin this evening at 8 p.m. You should report to wardroom around 7:30 p.m. for your adventure clothing. Now remember you and your wife will be going on an elk hunt your third day here."

After dinner Mr. and Mrs. Smith shower and dress for their events. "What fantasy did you select dear?" Asks Mavis.

"To be the winner at an international golfing tournament. What did you select?"

"I am going to scuba dive on that old mining town the first day and then get some professional tennis instructions on the second day."

Mark said, "I am so glad you found the ad for this Perfect Vacation."

"Yes, this is one that I will remember for the rest of my life."

The Elk Hunt

Mavis had never been so sexually active as she had been that last 48 hours. She met Mark in their room and had to forcibly act as energetic and focused as Mark appears to be. Mark also feels drained after the 48-hour sexual marathon but acts excited about his imaginary win at the golf tournament. "Let's hit the sack now to get an early start tomorrow morning. We're meeting a chuck wagon and the rest of our group at the outpost tomorrow morning at 8 a.m." They did not know that their drinks earlier were spiked with a delayed sleeping drug. During the night they were bundled up and taken to the site of the hunt.

Mavis is starting to stir and hears voices. She is covered and not able to move. "She won't make a good quarry. She doesn't have the physical strength or endurance. The hunting party would be disappointed. We had better put her into a calf roping event." A faraway woman's voice said.

"O.K. The man can still be the trophy hunt." Said the second voice.

A tarp is pealed off Mavis. Her hands and feet are tied and she is nude. She tries to yell out but tape covers her mouth. "Well, looks like sleeping beauty is awake. Help me cut the rope off her feet and get her up." Said Tex.

Looking over to a group of men, Mavis spots Jack. When the tape is painfully yanked off her mouth, she starts screaming for him. Glancing over, Jack sees Mavis and walks over to her.

"Jack what's going on. Get me loose. You have to help me."

"Sorry love, but it looks like you're going to be our entertainment."

"What do you mean entertainment?"

"You're going to be in a calf roping contest love." Said Jack.

The young teenage girl that helped Tex stand her up, said, "Tex, get her over to the cage while I get my horse into position."

Tex cut her foot restraints and yanked Mavis, in the direction of the rodeo arena, "Come on, get moving, we don't have all day."

"What are you doing? Where is my husband?"

"Oh, he'll be along shortly. Just do what your told and everything will be alright." And then Tex shoved Mavis

149

through a gate into a tall cage with a second gate facing the arena. "Cookie, are you in position?" He yelled.

"Hell yes." The teenager replied. "Turn her loose."

Tex released the rope tying her hands and said, "O.K. sweetie, get out and run like mad. You life depends on it."

Mavis stands frozen. Tex reached around and threw the arena side gate open. "Run girl, run. What's the matter with you."

"Dammit Tex, use the prod on her. Get her going."

Tex sticks a short tool through the bars that sparks and arced when he tries the button. Pushing the probe onto her bare buttocks sent an electrical charge through Mavis. She starts screaming and jumping before darting out and across the arena. About fifty feet out, she is yanked off her feet and pulled to the ground by a lasso thrown by Cookie. Leaping off her horse that pulled back on the rope, keeping the lasso tight, Cookie quickly wraps a cord around Mavis' wrists and then her ankles, throwing her hands up into the air to stop the seconds count. Mavis is hogtied and screaming like mad. The clapping response for the performance sounds like thunder.

150

Mavis is screaming, "Let me up, damn you. Let me up."

Cookie goes down to one knee. Her eyes brighten as she notices the detailed, beautiful rose tattoo on Mavis's butt. She pulls her sheath knife from her belt and deftly slices it off. Mavis shrieks from her pain. Cookie pays no attention to her pleading, yanks her head back by her hair and said, "Sorry, but you're scheduled for our evening meal," and then slowly slits her throat, then the cords that bind her. "Look Dad. I broke the record and she's barely bruised." Tex and Hank, another ranch hand, run out to retrieve Mavis, while the blood is still gushing from her neck, and roughly drag her off with ropes looped around her ankles. She is pulled below a gantry where her ankles are tied to a singletree and she is raised with block and tackle. Quickly drained of blood and field dressed she is lowered into a chill box. Cowboy butchers are consulting an old time recipe to complete the evening's menu.

Mark hears the crowd of people applauding, and is then uncovered and pulled from the rear of a truck. He see's the final seconds of Mavis' field dressing, removing her head. He almost faints, and then notices Jill smiling, sitting next to a man laughing. They both point in the direction of the slaughter. 'What's is going on?' He notices that he is not wearing any clothes, his hands are tied behind his back, and Tex is cutting the zip ties binding his wrists.

He tries to struggle, but two burly men held him. "You're getting a thirty minute head start, and then the hunting party will be coming after you. If you don't get away, you better hope for a quick kill. You don't want to be alive when they take their trophy." Said Tex.

"Hunting party? Trophy? What is happening? This has to be a nightmare."

Looking at his watch, Tex said, "Your time just started. You better start running." A look of horror swept across Mark's face, as he looks over to a small group gathered near some horses. Among them is Jill, snuggling against a man, tall and distinguished. They all carry rifles. "Run," said Tex, "or they will cut you up alive."

Mark took off running over the dusty ground, toward a grove of trees, the only possible protection he can see. Reaching the tree line brings disappointment. There is no cover. 'Maybe I can climb a tree and ambush one of the hunters, grab a rifle, and fight my way out of this.'

152

The hunting party begins their approach to the stand of trees. Scattering, they each are eager to claim their trophy. They are halfway through the grove when Mark leaps from a tree limb onto the back of a woman at the edge of the group that is examining his footprints in the dust. Viciously snapping her neck, he grabs her rifle. Before he has a chance to raise the rifle to fire, a bullet hits him in the neck.

Wounded, Mark drops to the ground. It isn't a mortal wound and he tries to crawl to some nearby shrubs. Jill is the first rider to reach him and dismounts. He watches her with fear as she pulls a long knife from her scabbard, kneels over him, removing her trophy as he feebly tries to protect himself. She stands, holding her bloody claim in the air yelling "Wahoo", while Mark writhes in pain.

Cookie walks toward Mark looking at a 'Mavis' tattoo. "Another one to add to my collection." Slicing off a thin section of skin, she carefully wraps it in a piece of cloth. Mark is still pleading when Cookie lightly sticks him a few times in the stomach, just for a reaction.

"Tex he's still kicking. Do you want me to finish him?"

Hank rides up, "No, I'll take care of him." While dismounting he congratulates Jill on her choice, and then approaches Mark with a fillet knife in hand. Working to remove his trophy from the shaking and moaning Mark, he said, "Easy guy, this won't take long and then your pain will be gone."

After approving Hank's trophy, and confirming his kill, Tex mounts his horse, and then orders another hand to load Mark onto a packhorse to take him back to the kitchen staff. "Tell them to clean him up good after he rolled around in all this dirt."

Jack was angrily complaining that he didn't get a trophy. "That was a dumb part of him to take. What the hell are you going to do with that?"

"Well, I'm going to have it pickled, so I have something worthwhile to look at when we get home." She replied.

"Dumb woman."

The Dinner

The chuck wagon cook did a superb job for dinner. There was enough of each cut to satisfy everyone. The left

154

over meat is taken back to the ranch to make Texas Chili for select guests. Jack said, "Dam, this is good. We should go on another hunt tomorrow." Everyone agreed. Later, after attending a party that went late, everyone settled down for the night.

The rising sun shines into Jill's eyes waking her. Her mouth is dry and she has a terrible headache. 'What a hangover.' She thought. Trying to move, she found herself bound and naked, lying next to Jack. Blankets covered both of them. "Jack. Wake up."

Jack opens his eyes and he too tries to move, only to find himself trussed up. "Hey, what's going on," he cries out.

Tex walks up, towering over them, blocking out the sun. "Well, you wanted another hunt, and since you two are well marinated from last night's drinking, we decided to accommodate your wishes."

"You can't do this, we're paying guests."

"Well, I talked to the boss, and he said, Nothing is better then hunting the hunter."

Cookie walked up smiling, patting her knife, and said, "I saw a video of you and that Mavis Smith. I selected then, my new trophy I'll be claiming today."

Another guest standing nearby added, "And I have been eying Jill all week. She has a lot to offer a guy that can bring her down and hogtie her. Cookie says she's not interested in a woman. Yep, she looks real tasty and it looks like she is all mine. I hope I get my money's worth out of her."

Uncle Max's Secret

My favorite uncle, Max, was a very secretive man. In his later years he often hinted that someday I would see him in a different light. He was inventive, creative and interesting.

After he died, his lawyer notified me, that the entire estate was willed to me, including intellectual properties. "What does this include?" I asked.

"I don't know." Replied the lawyer. "I was reviewing the last year's purchases that he made

157

and they included many strange items. Also, it appears, his land holdings include an old abandoned airfield in the Mojave Desert. As you read his will, he stipulates that as long as you continue his labor of love, you will continue to receive the dividends of his investments. You will be monitored by Elvira to ensure your compliance with these provisions. If Elvira determines that you are not living up to the spirit and letter of this instrument, all assets will be redirected to the charity of her choice."

"Who is Elvira?"

"I don't know, but apparently you will find out when she contacts you. Here are sealed envelopes that I have been instructed to give you, once you agree to the provisions of the will. If you agree, you will have to sign this formal document acknowledging your agreement."

"I feel there is no choice but to sign the paper."

An 11" X 14" manila envelope is passed to me when the document is completed with my signature. "I have been paid, to be your legal advisor for a period of twelve months, by your uncle's estate. Please do not hesitate to call on me for advice or legal action." The lawyer stands up, leaves the room and then his receptionist, who witnessed the proceedings, escorts me out of the office space.

All this is a surprise to me. Sure, Uncle Max and I were close, closer than any other relative. In fact he named me at birth, Matt. Our bond did create a little jealousy from my siblings, but nothing that could be considered aggressive.

Later that evening, I sit in a comfortable chair and begin reviewing the papers from the lawyer. Most did not make any sense when read randomly, but collating the individual packets spells out a sequence of instructions. I am to find the airport by following the directions that are spelled out from four different papers. There I will meet the mysterious Elvira. The intrigue written between the lines are overwhelming.

Four days later and four states away, I finally arrive at the airport in the dessert. It is indeed abandoned with derelict buildings. Hidden in plain view. The main hangar, apron and runway look in decent repair. Approaching the main hangar door, I notice an elaborate electronic security system with a hand-reading screen to gain access. 'What the heck, I might as well try it.' I thought. A red status light turns green and the door swung open. Only after entering and turning on lights did I realize how high tech the security is.

Turning away from the door I see an aircraft facing away from me toward a huge bank of mirrors. No, not mirrors, but windows on darkened rooms. The black room interiors give the windows the appearance of mirrors.

The aircraft is low riding on short wheel struts, swept back wings and twin tails. I had never seen such a craft. The skin appears shiny and mirror like, reminding me of Mylar. The hatch is open and inviting to my adventurous mind. Entering I walk the short distance to the cockpit in a crouch. None of the wrap-around instruments are labeled, but identified with letters across and numbers down. A keyboard panel is positioned to the left of a swivel pilot's seat. 'Nope, there is not an on/off switch.' I type "Matt" into the keyboard. A monitor screen comes to life and an incredibly beautiful woman's face looks back at me that zoom out to reveal a spectacular body dressed in formal dinner wear.

"Good morning Matt. Welcome to Excalibur One. My name is Elvira. Since Max is not available at this time, I will be your teacher, advisor, mentor and friend. You may ask me anything. How can I help you?"

"How do you know my name?"

"You are identified through facial recognition that Max incorporated into my logic and knowledge systems. Do you have more questions?"

"Yes. Just what is this craft?"

"This is a cloaking fighter and space craft?"

"Oh, this can't be real?"

"Yes Matt, this is real. Would you like a demonstration?"

"Yes, and Elvira, is it Miss or Mrs.?"

"It is neither. What demonstration would you like? Flight or cloaking?"

"I don't think that I am ready for flight, how about just demonstrating the cloaking."

"Nice choice Matt. If you will look at my reflection in the office windows, you will notice how nice I look."

"Yes, very nice. Now how about the cloaking?"

"Just hold on. I do not want to rush through all my mysterious assets. If you noticed, I am a woman. Keep watching the reflection."

The window reflection starts to shimmer, and then slowly fade away. An image of the hangar doors interior view suddenly appeared. "How is that possible?" I asked.

"It is quite simple. A 180-degree image is transmitted to a view angle. This is available from a 360-degree view. Would you like to view a video of my capabilities or physical attributes?"

Different thoughts crossed my mind as I ponder her offer. A playful smile came to Elvira's face. "Careful Matt. I can read your thoughts."

"Yes. I would like to see your video." For the next three hours I sit in amazement as the visual information played before me.

"Matt. My library of visuals covers any topic of my maintenance, operation or application. Everything about me can be accessed with voice recognition or I can be manually controlled. Also, I can be controlled by thought and can differentiate between random and controlling thinking. I am really something, right?"

"Yes, you are really something. I believe a well-deserved nap coming and when I awaken, we can take an orientation flight. How do I shut you down?"

"Oh, I cannot be shut down, but can be put into a standby status. Would you like for me to go to standby? And when shall I wake you?"

"Yes dear, go to standby and wake me in four hours."

"Yes Matt. Going to standby and will wake you in four hours."

It is a pitiful period of sleep. Fantasies about space travel and erotic dreams with a woman named Elvira. I should have been rested when awakened four hours later by a somewhat withdrawn and reserved Elvira. "Elvira. Did you read my dreams?"

"Yes Matt, I did. Luckily they did not compute with anything in my memory bank. I may ask for explanation and meaning at a later date. Are you ready for your first flight? Do you want stealth or space?"

"I think we'll start with stealth. Are you sure you cannot be seen by radar or other detectable sources?"

Yes Matt, I am sure. We will start warm up and take off in less than five minutes."

Matt hears a low hum and a slight vibration that slowly diminishes to nothing. All hangar lights are extinguished before the doors open. Elvira slowly exits the hangar and stops on the tarmac. "Matt, do you want standard or vertical take off?"

"Vertical will be fine."

"Yes Matt." A gentle pulsation is experienced as the craft takes off. Once in a hovering position at 500 feet, Elvira asks, "Matt, where would you like to go?"

"Surprise me."

Elvira responds by quickly accelerating to 1200 mph in an easterly route. "Elvira, I watched the video that explained your power plant and fuel source, but could you explain it to me again in a non-scientific manner?"

"Yes Matt. I carry one hundred gallons of liquid fuel, but can utilize any fuel source, liquid or gaseous. Once airborne a process of water vapor condensation occurs from air passing over warm fins and the water is collected in an insulated tank. This water is then broken down into oxygen and hydrogen through an application of electrical charge. This is known as hydrogen generation. The hydrogen is burned in a gaseous state and the chilled oxygen in re-introduced to the air through the exhaust from my power plant. The introduced oxygen returns the exhaust into near normal air temperature to avoid detection by heat, radar return, noise or visual."

"Thank you Elvira, that is a better explanation than the video."

We are soon over the Persian Gulf. Slowing down, we observe an aerial fight between a Russian and American fighter aircraft. "Elvira. Can we assist that American fighter? Maybe shoot down the Russian jet aircraft in pursuit of him?"

"Yes Matt. It is a simple matter to comply with your request."

"Do I have to do anything or can you do this on your own?"

"I will do everything. Should I contact the American aircraft to tell him we are interceding on his part?"

"No Elvira. We should fly silent and unobserved."

"Very well Matt."

In an instant, the Russian jet disintegrates in an explosion and falls to the earth. A view of the American canopy comes up on the monitor. The pilot looks around in confusion and his communication back to the carrier is overheard.

"I don't know what happened. I must have shot him down, but don't ask me how. I am returning   home   and   will   request   landing instructions at the fly by. Neptune's Lance out."

"Elvira. That really made me feel good. Why don't we return to our base?"

"Yes Matt, returning to base." In no time we circle our base and slowly settle on the tarmac. The hangar doors open for our entry and close while we are powering down. It is amazing how there is no jet blast or other turbulence.

'How did Uncle Max ever come up with this?' I thought.

Elvira, listening on my thoughts replied. "Max spent many years developing me. He was laughed at when he approached the military with his ideas. He told me that no one would ever get his inventions. There is a self-destruct application should my security ever get breached. If you would have not agreed to continue his work or if something were to happen to you, I would be no more as well as all his plans. There have been attempts to penetrate my barriers. All have been thwarted."

"Elvira. Who is your personality modeled after? I know Uncle Max was a bachelor, but did he ever have a love interest?"

"Yes Matt. Max did have a love interest that was not returned. She became a widowed single parent of a girl. I have been made in her image and personality. The particulars of her are not in my memory banks."

"Elvira. Can you find the particulars about her?"

"I will try."

"Boy, I am really hunga..."

"Matt, I am preparing a double hamburger and fries for you now. A cup of coffee will be ready in thirty seconds. I believe you like everything on your burger."

"Wonderful. Elvira, you would make any guy a terrific wife. After eating I will take a nap. And Elvira, please do not listen on my dreams."

"I will try not to listen in." A soft giggle is heard as the communication circuit fades out.

Matt is awakened. It is near midnight and sleep shakes off slowly. Elvira announces that she has all the information on the woman she is modeled on. "Matt. I have found the woman you asked me to research. She is twenty-six, just one year younger than you. She has never been married or even engaged. There are two remarkable things that stand out about her."

"What are they Elvira?"

"Well, believe it or not, her name is also Elvira and she looks just like me."

Laughing I said. "Just like you the aircraft?"

"No, silly. Just like my image on the monitor, but I can appear in any form of clothing or in any environment that I wish. I don't think she can do that."

"We will have to arrange a chance meeting, won't we?"

Elvira appears to pout. "Don't worry Elvira. You will always be my favorite aircraft and monitor image. And don't forget that you are my teacher, advisor, mentor and very close friend."

"Really."

"Yes, definitely."

Bed And Breakfast

The newspaper classified ad read, "Bed and Breakfast - $50 per day; $250 Per Week. Linens changed daily. Lunch and Supper are available at reasonable prices. All major modes of transportation are within walking distance. Located at the edge of town in a wooded setting. Private Bath. Free HD Television and Wi-Fi included. Wooded hiking trails available. A few quiet and secluded suites are available by reservation only. Room service requires a surcharge. Call 555-5455 for additional information. Ask for Helen. "

'This is just what I need, a vacation from my hectic pace. This is something I can do.' Putting her morning coffee down and picking up the cell she punches in the number.

On the second ring a melodious voice answered. "Smith's Bed & Breakfast, how can I help you?"

"Is the price that ran in this morning's *Dailey Informant* correct? I am reading $250 per week plus lunch and supper, and are there any of the quiet and secluded suites still available?"

"Yes, we have two available. One in a corner wing of the second floor and one, a detached cabin, about 300 feet into the woods. And yes, that price is correct."

"Can you reserve the cabin for me. I can be there this afternoon. My name is Hhhmmmmm Marilyn Jones. And I hope cash will be O.K. "

"Cash will be fine, and is it Miss or Mrs. Jones."

"Miss."

Arriving in the early afternoon, Miss Jones stands at the reception desk marveling at the size of the mansion and the décor. 'I cannot believe they can offer all this that cheaply. I may just chuck my life away and start over here. This is absolutely beautiful', she thought to herself.

A man and woman, neatly dressed, stands behind the counter. "May we help you?"

172

"Yes. I am Miss Marilyn Jones. I called this morning for a cabin reservation. I am looking forward to a week of undisturbed rest where I can just relax and write. Will I be able to take all my meals in the cabin?"

"Yes, the meals can be delivered to the cabin. Every night the next day's menu will be placed in the mailbox for you to select from. Most of our clientele are repeat patrons of our establishment. In fact, we have permanent residents that take their evening meal in a private building, not too far from your cabin, but do not worry, you will not be disturbed. We do require advance payment for the cabin, and I have a note here that you want to pay in cash. I take it that you have not told anyone of your stay here since you preferred seclusion."

"No one knows I'm here and I would like to keep that way."

"You'll have complete privacy. I will need a name, address and telephone number of a responsible party in case of an emergency. Just place the information here below your entry in the registry book."

Marilyn thought of a bogus name, address and telephone number to use, and carefully recorded that information in the book. Reviewing other entries, she could see that this outfit did a brisk business, and thought, "I'll have to remember this place, after I take on another sucker to drain his accounts." Without thinking, she casually patted the overnight bag that never leaves her side. It held over $500,000.

A house worker was called to wheel the luggage out to the cabin. "She really is a striking red head," said John to Helen, his companion.

"Just forget it, that's not why she is here. Keep your mind on track to the business we run here."

The cabin looked very comfortable. Fully furnished with a cozy fireplace. The man brought in her luggage and asked, "Would you like me to start a fire?"

"No, but I could use a sandwich and cup of coffee. I missed lunch today," laughed, and said, "I need to keep my strength up."

The man laughed and said, "I will check what is available in the kitchen. I'm sure there is some roast beef for an open faced sandwich"

"That would be wonderful, thank you."

John Smith put down the telephone, smiled, and looked at Helen. "Everything was bogus, just like we thought. Looks like everything is a go, and with perfect

174

timing too. We were running low on supplies at our dinner club. "

Marilyn was recounting her money, enjoying the snack. "Another ten foolish men and I'll be able to retire early. Being young really is the best. Those old farts fall all over themselves trying to get close to me." Stripping off her clothes, she studied her twenty two year old body in the mirror before slipping down into the hot bubbly water. Finishing her bath, she poured a glass of the complimentary wine then sat in a cushy love seat to relax. Sleep came over her quickly, from the drugged wine, as she dreamed of the money that would come her way and the enjoyment received from the creative games played with all the over the-hill-men in her future. She did not hear the two men enter the cabin, or feel them carefully place her on a gurney and take her to the nearby building used by the dinner club.

Twelve club couples were gathered to partake in the evening's dinner. "This crown rib roast is the best ever. I'm buying into a lifetime membership if the food continues like this." Looking down, he studies the place mat photo of the nude, unconscious, red haired woman, hanging upside down, in the small butcher shop behind the kitchen. "It's a shame, a young good looking woman like that, but boy is she ever tender" he commented to the server. Returning his attention to the place mat, he debated what cut he would order the next evening.

Read The Prologue

And First Chapter

From

The Palace of Virtual Reality

By Charles Schwend

Available Now At Major

Book Stores

And

Amazon

Prologue

Somewhere in Ancient Britannia

Oh God, hear my words. Let me die now and not suffer for eternity. I do not deserve to languish in this insufferable hell of darkness and solitude. I have prayed for even the smallest spark of light to postpone the insanity that has befallen me. This blanket of blackest night has stopped time. I know not if my confinement has been days, weeks, months, years, or centuries. My powers have dwindled to nothing. I feel I am nothing more than a memory of a memory.

I was Merlin the Great. I had planned to create a world of peace and happiness, and now I am less than a grain of sand. How could have I been so foolish to let Niviane, the Lady of the Lake, trap and imprison me in this inescapable black vault of rock? She was more beguiling than the sweetest flower until she learned all that I knew. How could I have known what her ulterior motives were, before my sudden betrayal suffered at her hands? Her sinister actions turned my heart cold.

Even now, knowing what I do, with my demise imminent, I feel my actions, my mistakes leading to my present confinement, would only be repeated. As I feel my remaining essence, from the smallest part of my being, slip away, I know that I will be no more. My only consolation is that my manuscript, holding the records of myself and that of all the ancient gods will someday be discovered. Everything about the gods and I, all the physical descriptions and details of mental psyche and design, recorded for the inheritors of the world to view. Maybe then, just maybe, our deeds and thoughts will again enlighten the world.

I am tired of my cruelly imposed existence, and must now relinquish myself to the eternal sleep. I ....

Chapter 1

In a secluded rural New England mansion, an old man leans over an electronic control panel, his white hair long and unruly, talking to himself. His jerky body motions coordinate with a spastic speech pattern. High-pitch giggles and half spoken words heighten the scene of a mad doctor in a futuristic science laboratory. A tattered old leather bound book lay open, pages yellowed with age, on the flat platform before the wild looking venerable man. A twisted sinewy finger follows scripted code lines of information, while data is entered on a keyboard embedded in a soft-lit control panel.

His eyes pan over the room with proud satisfaction. The equipment resembles giant vacuum tubes ten foot tall, and glass drums fifteen-foot long rest horizontally on massive cradles. Humming control panels, computers, monitors, a row of wired containers that could be mistaken for old fashion caskets stand upright, and everything looking like it came out of a sci-fi museum.

Dials are turned and numbers keyed in on an array of panel buttons. Banks of digital readouts and sine waves on oscilloscope displays are monitored. A larger, more prominent button, marked *Review* is slowly pressed. A turbulent mist forms in an upright tube. Miniature jagged streaks of lightning crackle and pop through the cloudy mass.

From the misty cloud in the large upright cylindrical glass container, a hologram takes form of an elderly man, with stately features, intelligence and knowledge reflecting in his face. "Yes. Yes," screams the bizarre looking man standing at the control panel. He throws levers, and pushes more buttons with uncontrollable excitement. Then with hesitation, the button marked *Finish* is pressed. The mist slowly swirls, and then clears. In another horizontal glass tube, a more substantial image forms. Cloudy gas boils around the core matter reposed on a surface bed of white marble. A jagged leap of electricity arcs through the chamber, illuminating the room with a stark bright flash. A liquid mist gently washes away the cloudy mist, revealing the elderly man as a solid, humanly fleshed being. A light breeze blows from head to toe, drying the man. His forehead wrinkles and lips twitch. Thick black hair waves in the circulating air.

A quiet release of pressure emanates from the tube as a circular end cap, the door, opens near his feet. The platform bed slowly and quietly slides out on rails, exposing the naked man to the electrically charged atmosphere of the room.

The man at the control panel becomes ecstatic. Leaping to his feet he shouts out. "I did it, I did it. I knew it would work." Running to the prone man, he softly says. "Merlin, can you hear me? Open your eyes."

Merlin slowly opens his eyes and looks up at this wild looking man hovering over him. "Where am I? Who are you?"

"Get up. Stand. Let me look at you."

I must not be dead. God is punishing me with this nightmare. I am still imprisoned. He looks at his surroundings, trying to gather his senses, to orientate himself to this new challenge.

The insane looking man grabs Merlin by the wrists, yanks him up to a sitting position, then to his feet. "Look. Look at you. You are perfect."

"Where am I? Who are you?" asks Merlin again. "What is this language I speak and how do I know it?"

"You are in America, a country that was unknown in your time. It is the year 2016. I am Professor Ambrose Hamlock. What you are speaking is modern English that was programmed into your memory, as you were being re-created. Come look at yourself. Look at what I have done. Look, look." He pulls Merlin onto a rotating turntable surrounded with tall mirrors.

Merlin stares at his reflection. *This wild man, this Professor Hamlock must also be a magician. My image is perfect.* Then Merlin inspects his reflection closer. A younger man reflects back then when he was imprisoned. *I am truly free.* Slowly rotating in the center of the mirrors Merlin realizes that this is the first time he has viewed himself with such clarity. His head turns to focus and follow Professor Hamlock, to study him. "You are a great magician. You have rescued me from my prison."

"No, not rescued, re-created. I have re-created you. Come, now we must clothe and feed you. Come with me." Professor Hamlock leads the confused Merlin toward a large wardrobe.

Walking past the working platform, Merlin recognizes his book on the gods and he from long ago, the script is faded on the yellowed pages. He carefully dresses himself with the oversized clothes provided, while keeping a suspicious eye on the old man.

"I did not know your desire for fit or size, so I went big for comfort."

"It is suitable," replies Merlin, then let himself be led to a large dining area where a table is filled with foods he does not recognize. Servers stand by, waiting to accommodate the needs of the new guest.

"We have many things to talk about, but that can wait until after we eat and you have rested," said Professor Hamlock.

"I would think I have rested enough. How many years have I been sleeping, waiting for my rescue?"

"Not rescued, re-created. Merlin, I have not rescued you. I re-created you from out of thin air. You are the first of many. The gods described in your book will soon follow you to the present. You will, of course, advise me on what positive attributes of the gods to enhance and what negative aspects need to be diminished. You will be my right hand."

Merlin did not like being referred to as a right hand, an assistant or a secondary to an authority, *even to one who did not rescue him, but re-created him. Yes, I must patronize this powerful magician.* "Yes, I can see I have much to learn from you, and I will assist you in your endeavors."

"Merlin you cannot realize how your words humble me. With our joined minds, we can accomplish anything."